1841-1930 Pansy

Mary Burton and other Stories

A Book for Girls

1841-1930 Pansy

Mary Burton and other Stories
A Book for Girls

ISBN/EAN: 9783744749770

Printed in Europe, USA, Canada, Australia, Japan

Cover: Foto ©Andreas Hilbeck / pixelio.de

More available books at **www.hansebooks.com**

MARY BURTON

AND

OTHER STORIES

A Book for Girls.

————

BOSTON:
THOMAS B. NOONAN & CO.
1884.

Electrotyped and Printed by
CASHMAN, KEATING & CO.
603 Washington St., Boston.

CONTENTS.

3

MARY BURTON.

IT is many years ago that I went one
morning, at the request of the clergy-
man of my parish, to undertake the teaching
of a class of Sunday scholars.   As I entered
the room, in which my duties were in future
to be performed every Sunday morning,
the nervous feeling which had been gathering strength as I walked along, almost overcame me, and I think I should have turned
and run home again, had not the kind clergy-
man caught sight of my anxious face, and
come forward to encourage me.

"That is right, Miss Smith," he said, as he shook hands with me. "I am glad you have consented to comply with my wishes, and to take a class here."

"If I could only teach them right," I answered timidly; "but I feel as if I should be better employed in learning than in teaching." -

"You have been learning for many months past," he answered kindly, "learning from higher than mere human teaching, learning in the school of sorrow and of suffering. Let it be seen that the lesson has not been sent in vain. Strive to lead others to that gracious Saviour, whom you have yourself learned to love, and who said, 'Suffer little children to come unto Me.'"

He led me to a class of little girls seated at the further end of the room, and left me with them. I glanced at the faces turned inquisitively towards the "new teacher." I will relate the subsequent history of one of these children, whose appearance particularly impressed me.

Mary Burton was a fair-haired, blue-eyed girl, with an expression of contentment on her face, which made it pleasant to look at her. She was eleven years old, she told me, and lived with her mother, who was a widow. I made a point of becoming acquainted with my children in their own homes; and as Mary was never in during the week, being employed as a message-girl at a neighboring green-grocer's, I went one Sunday, after afternoon service, to see her. I found the family seated at tea. Everything was neat and clean; and the mother, in her widow's dress and cap, looked the picture of decent and respectable poverty. She told me she had been seven years a widow, and that her youngest child (she had three) had been born two months after his father's death.

"I have had a hard struggle to keep things straight, ma'am," she said; "but now that Mary is growing up to be a help and comfort to me, I feel as if a great burden was taken off me; for I know that she will do what she can to work for her mother, and that, as long as she lives, her brothers will not want for a good example and good advice." Mary's face was flushed with pleasure at her mother's praise, and at the few words of encouragement which I gave her.

As I rose to take my leave, I said, "I will leave you a maxim to think about, Mary. It is this: 'Godliness with contentment is great gain.' God has blessed you with a naturally contented disposition, but something more is needed. May you, like Mary of old, be enabled to choose that good part, which shall never be taken from you."

When Mary was fourteen years old her mother was taken very ill. It was a painful and lingering disease, borne with such meek patience as taught a sweet lesson of faith and trust to all who were privileged to see her in her affliction. Mary came home to look after the invalid and her two little brothers, and it was then that her mother found the blessing of having "trained up her child in the way it should go." Early accustomed to orderly habits and to hard work, it was wonderful how that young girl contrived to keep everything about the poor invalid clean and comfortable, to have the room always tidy, and her brothers' clothes well washed and mended.

They had many difficulties and hardships. The boys could only earn five dollars a week between them, and this did not allow food sufficient for three growing and hard-worked children, and the round faces became blue and pinched; still there was no murmuring, or parade of want. Go when I would, Mary was busy with her work, and, amid all their poverty, kept up an appearance of comfort, by her clean and tidy ways.

One day I remember I found her with a face unusually pale, and the evident traces of tears in her eyes.

"What is the matter, Mary?" I said.

She made a sign towards her mother's bed, as if to beg me not to draw attention to her distress, and answered, as she dusted a chair and placed it near the bed for me,

"Nothing, ma'am; I think mother's keeping pretty well just now."

Her mother had turned anxiously around as I asked the question; but Mary had so naturally contrived her answer, placing herself at the same time in a position which should conceal her face without an apparent intention to do so, that Mrs. Burton was satisfied. It was my practice, when I visited the widow, to read a chapter aloud, which we talked over afterwards. Her religion was not a mere talk; it was a real possession. She *knew* "in whom she could trust;" and, in her hour of trial, of bodily suffering, and often of actual want, she would carry her trials and troubles to her Saviour, and, laying the burden at His feet rest contented in the assurance, "The Lord will provide." She was generally a woman of few words; but that day she spoke more than was her wont, and, among other things, reminded me of the maxim which I had left with Mary on my first visit to them.

"It has often been a comfort to me since,"

she said, "and I am sure I find the truth of it more and more every day. To know that our daily-bread comes direct from our Father's hands, seems to make it taste the sweeter; and when things have gone harder than usual, and I could see no way how we could get help, the help has come often in a way that I least expected, till I have been made to feel that to be content with what the Lord is pleased to give us, and to see and know that all comes from His loving hands, is indeed the greatest gain."

I observed that as she spoke, Mary rather paused in her work, and at last she left off altogether, and stood looking out of the window, while her hands hung listlessly at her side. It may be easily supposed that I did not usually go to the house empty-handed. I have little sympathy with the piety which leads some really good people to visit the houses of the poor, to read to them, and to give them tracts, and to over-look their bodily wants and suffering al-together. Such, at all events, was not the practice of " Him who has left us an example that we should follow his footsteps."

It had not pleased God to endow me largely with worldly goods, but it does not require large means to enable one to be kind and helpful to the poor. If we bring a willing heart to the work, we shall soon find many ways at helping, at no greater cost than some slight personal inconvenience or self-denial. That day I had in my purse a five-dollar piece which a wealthy friend, to whom I had spoken of the widow's patient suffering, had given me for her use. As I saw that something had gone wrong with Mary, and that she was anxious to conceal her distress from her mother, I determined on speaking to her when she accompanied me to the outer door, which she usually did, and that I would give her the money then.

Mary looked nervous when I rose to go away, and as if she would be glad of an excuse for not accompanying me. She saw however, that I expected her, and followed with a slow, unwilling step. When we were quite out of her mother's hearing, I stopped.

" There is something vexing you, Mary," I said, " and I suspect you do not want to tell me what it is. If it would be any comfort to speak to a true friend about your troubles, I would willingly hear what is the matter; but if you would rather not tell me, I shall not feel hurt."

I waited a moment, and as she remained silent, I added, —

" I see you would rather not; but remember, dear Mary, that there is One whose ear is ever open to our cry, who is ever ready to pity and to help us. Tell your trouble to Him — ask His guidance if you are in difficulty — cast your care upon Him if you are in trouble, and be assured that none who go in simple trust to Him, shall be sent empty away."

She answered, —

" Oh, Miss Smith, I have prayed, indeed I have, but," —

" But it seems to you as if the Lord had

not heard your prayer," I said, finishing her sentence for her. " He does not always answer us in the way that we expect; we are poor blind creatures, and do not know what to ask for as we ought; but be assured that the prayer of faith will be answered; if not in the way we wish, at any rate in the way that will be best for us. I will not detain you any longer from your mother," I added; " she may wonder what is keeping you. Here is a small sum which a friend gave me for you. I have seen that you are to be trusted with money, and that you are thoughtful and prudent in spending the little you have; so I feel sure you will lay this out to the best advantage."

She looked at me with an eagerness in her large blue eyes that quite startled me; clasped her hands together, and for some minutes remained silent; then she burst into a fit of passionate, almost hysterical weeping, which shook her the more, that she endeavored to suppress all sound. When she was a little composed, she explained the cause of her agitation. Her elder brother, whose earnings brought three dollars a week to the family, had completely worn out his shoes and his clothes, and his master had more than once threatened to dismiss him unless he were better clad. Poor Mary had almost denied herself necessary food, in the endeavor to lay by a sufficient sum to buy him a pair of shoes; but meanwhile, in spite of constant mending, his clothes had become so worn that they would scarcely hold together, and on Monday, his master had warned him that this must be his last week, unless he came better clothed. Friday had come, and Mary was as far as ever from having obtained money for so extensive a purchase, and saw no means of getting it, and hence arose her anxious, careworn looks.

"I could not tell mother," she said, "for the doctor says she must not be fretted; it might cost her her life."

"And why could you not tell me?" I answered.

“ Oh ! ma’am, I thought shame, when you have done so much for us already ; ’twould have been begging like.”

She was crying still, for the poor child was weak for want of sufficient food ; so I said, soothingly, —

“ You went to the right quarter, Mary, and He, whose kind heart, when he was on earth, never allowed Him to despise the cry of the weakest or poorest, has proved that He is ‘ the same yesterday, to-day, and for-ever.’ As surely does this help come from Him, though through my hand, as when in olden times He commissioned the ravens to feed the prophet, or multiplied the five loaves and two small fishes into food for five thousand fainting followers.”

“ Yes, ma’am, I feel it now. Mother often told me to trust in Him ; but somehow I thought I was such a weak, wicked creature, He could never listen to me ; but now I feel as if I could never doubt Him again, for it seems as if He had sent you o’ purpose to help us in our great need.”

And, indeed, from that time she seemed able to cast her whole care upon her Saviour God. She had. been contented before; her training and natural temperament had made her so; but now a higher element was added —a simple trust in her heavenly Father's love and care, an earnest faith in the redemption purchased by the blood of His dear Son, with the abiding presence of that Comforter, whose offices of love were the Saviour's dying bequest to His people, filled her heart, and constituted that godliness which, with contentment, she truly found to be great gain.

Some months later Mrs. Burton died.

Mary had dearly loved her mother, and had looked up to her in everything for advice. It was a bitter loss, but she bore it with sweet, unmurmuring patience.

"I know she is happy now," she said, as she uncovered the pale face, and her hot tears dropped fast upon it. "I must try to remember all she used to tell me, but, oh! I can never be like her, so good, so patient."

We can say little in the face of death; those

white, silent lips are far more eloquent than ours; they speak to the bereaved in a language which the mere spectator neither hears nor understands, so I thought it kinder to leave Mary to her Saviour and her great sorrow.

When I returned the following day she was herself again, quite composed and calm. It had been her mother's earnest wish that Mary should, if possible, keep house for her brothers.

It was not easy, but she effected it; she was clever and I was fortunate in interesting an excellent woman in the neighborhood in her case. This woman was a clear-starcher; she taught Mary her business without any charge and gave her constant employment. Her brothers' earnings, too, increased as they grew older; so that, after a time, they lived in comparative comfort.

When Mary was twenty years of age, she married a farmer, who lived about five miles out of town. Her elder brother had obtained an excellent situation through his steadiness and good character. This enabled him to go into comfortable and respectable lodgings, and his younger brother went to live with him. They were both excellent, steady lads, and in a fair way to get on in the world.

It was fully four years after Mary's marriage that I one day resolved to make her a visit, which she had earnestly pressed upon me before she left the home where I had first known her. I availed myself of a coach which took me to within two miles of the village where Mary lived, and walked the rest of the way.

My path lay through corn-fields and green lanes, and I thoroughly enjoyed the contrast afforded by the pleasant sights and sounds of the country with the bustle and turmoil of dirty and crowded streets. A neat cottage, with a pretty garden in front of it, was pointed out to me as Mary's home. I was prepared for order and cleanliness, but scarcely for the almost elegant comfort that pervaded the room. The furniture was of the plainest description, but there was an exquisite neatness, and even taste, in its arrangement, which made one feel that the mistress of such a house was no ordinary person.

Mary herself was there, with a baby on her knee, and a pretty little creature, two years old, playing near her on the floor. She greeted me with a happy smile.

"Oh! ma'am," she said, "this is kind. I have longed so to show you my new home, and my little ones!"

"And I often wished to come," I answered; "but, as you know, I have a great deal at home to occupy my time, and when I have planned to come, something has occurred to prevent me."

It was a pleasant visit. We spoke of her mother and of past times, of her present circumstances and future prospects.

"Oh, ma'am," she said, and grateful tears filled her eyes, "I feel as if I never can be thankful to my Father in heaven for all His goodness. Of course, we have had our troubles at times, and, worst of all, was when my little baby died, our first, when it was six months old; but, through all, we seem to have had so much comfort and peace, as if the Lord, Himself, was comforting and strengthening us. So that I am sure we have reason to say, 'Bless the Lord, O my soul, and forget not all His benefits.'"

"Ah, Mary," I answered, as I rose to go, "you know now, by happy experience, that 'Godliness with contentment is great gain.'"

As I walked home that beautiful summer evening, watching the golden sunset, and the purple hue of declining day stealing over hill and valley, and thought of Mary with her sweet face and quiet happiness and peace, these words came to my mind,—

"God hath appointed one remedy for all the evils in this world, and that is — a contented spirit."

ZOE; OR, THE METAMORPHOSIS.

CHAPTER I.

THE SORCERER.

"HADZIUN a Poun!"

"Hadziun a Poun!"

"Hadziun a Poun!"

These magic words were pronounced in a terrible voice, one winter evening, by an old man, of a gloomy and malevolent aspect. He wore a high, pointed, black silk hat, and a long, black old gown that reached to his feet. Seated on a curiously-formed stool, he

23

turned persistently the handle of a vessel in
which something extraordinary seemed to be
boiling. This old man was not a confec-
tioner, and they were not cakes or creams of
which he took such care ; he was not making soup, or panoda, or anything you could
imagine. The old fellow was a sorcerer,
dear children, a wise man, but a wicked man
at the same time ; that is to say, one who
employed his knowledge to do evil, just as
good men use science to ameliorate the condition of mankind.

This sorcerer had read somewhere of
another sorcerer, who had, by means of his
arts, formed a man out of clay, bones, and
ashes, and who had animated the senseless
mass by the use of certain magic words. He
had taken it upon himself to imitate the work
of his fellow-magician ; but instead of a man
he had proposed forming a woman, and he
already began to hope for the success of his
enterprise.

The saucepan had now been on the fire
sixty-three days, sixty-three nights, three

minutes, and three seconds, and he began to anticipate happy results. At each inspection of its contents, the sorcerer had been satisfied with their progress; the twenty-first day he lifted the pot from the fire, and, placing it on the ground, pronounced the following words:

"Hadziun a Poun!"

"Hadziun a Poun!"

"Hadziun a Poun!"

He was filled with delight to see a jolly little mouse jump from the saucepan and run around the room. He caught it immediately, threw it back into the pan, and put on fresh fire. Several days afterward he essayed a second proof; this time it was a weasel.

"Good!" he exclaimed, "it is coming; I am making great progress. In ten days I shall have a rabbit, then a cat, then a woman! Good, good!" and he rubbed his hands together with joy.

Remember that he was a sorcerer, and that he had only power to create a wicked woman; otherwise, he would have begun

by making a bee, then a swallow, then a
dove, then a gazelle, and at length a sweet
young girl.   That is what a good man would
have done.

The sorcerer stirred his mixture all night,
with a gold spoon, on the end of which was
a silver hand, with sparkling little rings on
the fingers.   He stirred and stirred, until,
exhausted by fatigue, about daybreak he
threw himself on his old sofa and slept.

CHAPTER II.

THE LILAC DRESS.

THE same day, at the same hour, a little girl, who lived in the next house, awoke from sleep.

"Rosa," said she to her nurse, "it will be a fine day; I do not want to put on my old black gown; I would like to wear that pretty lilac frock my aunt has given me."

"Miss Zoe," answered Rosalie, "your lilac frock is not ironed yet; I only washed it yesterday."

"Well, iron it then," replied Zoe, in an imperious tone.

"That is impossible, miss; there is not a fire in any part of the house."

"Bah!" cried out the little girl, impatiently; "you always have good reasons for not doing what you are told."

With these words, Zoe got up, and after a few moments, went down stairs. She perceived a fire and smoke in the sorcerer's great chimney, and he had left the door of the laboratory open, so as not to be stifled by the great quantity of burning charcoal.

Zoe was a forward little girl who hesitated at nothing, when she wished to gratify her caprices. She passed, without being seen, the wide court which separated her from the sorcerer's abode, and, finding herself all alone, she entered the mysterious laboratory.

At the aspect of the motionless old man, she recoiled with fear; for he looked extremely wicked, although tired and asleep. But this fear was soon dissipated, and Zoe approached the furnace. Her desire was to obtain a few coals to heat an iron or two; and, while she was fearful of awaking the sorcerer, she had, at the same time, determined to wear her lilac frock. She scarcely dared breathe, so frightened was she, — but her lilac frock, her lilac frock, — she must wear it, for it was her mamma's birthday, and some of her little friends were coming to spend the day. She was very vain, this little Zoe, and she had often been told that her vanity would some day or other be a cause of misfortune to her. She succeeded at length in getting some red coals from the fire with the tongs, and was about to steal softly out, when she saw two terrible eyes looking at her from the bottom of the magic saucepan.

Her terror was so great that she uttered a loud cry, and the tongs dropped from her grasp. At the same instant, the sorcerer awoke.

CHAPTER III.

THE METAMORPHOSIS.

ONE must have spent some years on a work, or an idea, to comprehend the importance which a man attaches to his labor, a painter to his picture, a poet to his verses, a *savant* to a discovery. Children never understand this; they attach importance to trifles only, and break them as soon as they have received them. However, children who have been well brought up know better, and respect that of which they are ignorant.

Zoe was not aware that she had, in depriving the saucepan of the requisite heat, destroyed the labor of months that the sorcerer had vainly toiled night and day to accomplish results now impossible. Imagine her terror and the despair of the old man. He became pale with anger; he wept with rage — the rage of a sorcerer; the tears fell upon his white beard, and he wrung his hands with grief. He could not speak, but he repeated in his mind the most terrible imprecations, the most powerful maledictions against the poor child who had fallen on her knees before him, uplifting her trembling hands.

All at once, raising his head, and as though seized with an inspiration of vengeance, he grasped the fatal vessel in which she had seen the terrible eyes, and violently threw its contents in Zoe's face, who fell to the ground in a paroxysm of terror and pain.

The sorcerer, walking around her prostrate figure several times, pronounced the following words :

"Hadziun a Poun ! "

"Hadziun a Poun ! "

"Hadziun a Poun ! "

" Hadziun a Poun ! "

And Zoe was Zoe no longer; her pretty little hands were changed into paws with long claws; her soft blue eyes, into big, ugly, green eyes; her light, silky hair into short fur. Poor Zoe, so dainty, so proud of her beauty, was only a great cat, without grace or prettiness of any kind.

When the unfortunate child returned to herself and began to understand this metamorphosis, her heart grew very sad. She wished to speak in the childish voice which her dear mother never could resist; but, alas! she had no voice, — she *meawed*, but she *meawed* falsely; for the sorcerer, who had never before made a cat, had not given her even such a pleasant voice as the finest cats possess, and her sad complaints were without sweetness.

You remember the last trial was to be a cat, before arriving at a woman, and this cat did not give great promise of the woman who was to succeed her; it was probable she would be very grossly constructed, and that

her voice would be quite destitute of charms.
Observing all this, as he could not help
doing, and comparing her wails to the dis-
cordant notes of a broken music-box, the
sorcerer did not enjoy hearing the cracked
voice that did him so little honor. While
Zoe complained, she heard her maid in the
court-yard, calling her. "Zoe, Zoe," re-
sounded on all sides, and the poor cat
bounded up and down the room in the greatest anguish.

"Ha! ha!" cried the wicked sorcerer,
with a demoniacal laugh: "hear them calling
you, my little cat; your mother will be delighted to see you in your new clothes. Ha,
ha! what a beautiful costume! This new
dress feels a little strange in the beginning;
but you will be well used to it, for you will
never be rid of it until some one says, 'Zoe,
I pardon you!' and certes, that shall never
be I." With these words, the sorcerer gave
her a blow with his foot, which sent her into
the court-yard, where she lay for a moment
almost stunned.

CHAPTER IV.

EVERY ONE DOES NOT LOVE CATS.

"ZOE, Zoe, breakfast is ready!"

"Miss Zoe, Madame is calling you. Have you seen Zoe, M. Pechor," said the waiting-maid to the porter.

"No, Miss, I have not seen her to-day."

"Zoe, Zoe," and Zoe ran to the vestibule at the sound of her name; she ventured to enter the dining-room, when her nurse seeing her, gave her a blow, saying:

"Ah, what a sight; where did that ugly cat come from? Clear out, this instant. I do not like cats; there is nothing I hate like a cat. Pusch! Pouah! Pouah! Clear away." And poor Zoe was obliged to go away.

As she sadly descended into the hall, she met her little cousin carrying a large basket of confectionaries, which she was bringing to share with her.

" Zoe, Zoe," cried the little girl, " come to breakfast, quick ; we have got candy."

Zoe, forgetting that she was a cat, approached her cousin, and wished to take the basket from her ; but the little girl began to scream at the top of her voice, " Mamma, mamma, here is a big cat trying to eat my candies."

The unhappy cat was forced to wander about sadly, very sadly, without having anything to eat. She went to her own room, and lay down on the bed, hoping for security there, at least. But she had hardly settled herself when her nurse entered. She carried in her hand the lilac frock, freshly ironed — the fatal robe that had caused so much misery. " Zoe," said she, " come, Zoe, do not pout ; come and dress yourself ; your dress is ready, come."

Rosalie sought the little girl behind the

door.and in all the corners, imagining that she had hidden herself; seeking and calling her from side to side, she threw here and there various things that lay in her way; then she began to take off the covering to make the bed. In lifting the spread she saw the cat, at which discovery she grew very angry.

"You are here yet, are you, ugly beast!" she exclaimed. "What are you doing there? *Will* you go away!" and "*pusch, pusch, pusch*" began once more, accompanied with kicks, and blows of the broom.

Zoe, terribly frightened, ran away as quickly as possible, and, fleeing from the awful wrath of Rosalie, she threw herself before her mother's door, and awaited her awaking with something like resignation. "In spite of this dreadful change," she said to herself, "mamma will certainly know me; oh, I am sure she will recognize me; she will understand me; she will hear me although I cannot speak, if I can only be near her. She loves me so dearly, she will not allow them to harm me."

CHAPTER V.

A SAD BIRTHDAY.

WHILE Zoe crouched, trembling, by the door, she saw her two little cousins skipping up the corridor, beautifully dressed, their faces beaming with joy. When they came close to her mamma's chamber, they walked on tip-toe, each holding a bouquet in her little hand.

"Auntie is not awake yet," said one; "we cannot wish her a happy feast. Where is Zoe? She will put our bouquets in water."

"Miss Zoe is in her room," replied a servant who was passing, ignorant of what had transpired.

"Ah, I know," answered the elder of the two. "I know. She is arranging her curls; I ought to know that she will be very particular about her dress to-day. I have been ready since eight o'clock."

With these words, she produced a pretty pair of mittens which she had knitted for her aunt. Zoe saw all these things, these presents, the bouquets, and her poor heart beat sorrowfully. On her side it was not that she feared having nothing to give her mamma; her bouquet and souvenir were ready long ago — but to be obliged to present them with the paws of a cat!

At this moment she felt very unhappy, but that was not enough. At the end of an hour, her mother rang the bell, and when her maid answered the summons, Rosalie ran after her in a perspiration.

"If Madame asks for Miss Zoe," said she, " say that she has gone with me to buy flowers. That will give me time to search for her; we do not know what has become of her. Ah! *mon Dieu! mon Dieu!*" she exclaimed; "I shall die if anything has happened to her!"

Zoe, miserable at seeing her nurse weeping on account of her absence, wished to console her, and, forgetting that she could not speak, arose and advanced towards her; but Rosalie repulsed her, this time, however, without blows; for the poor girl was so uneasy that she had not time to be cross.

The alarm soon spread throughout the household, and no one was able to hide the anxiety that manifested itself. Madame Epernay, not seeing her daughter return, and noticing the mysterious actions and evasive answers of the servants, began to suspect that something was wrong. She hastened to the chamber of her daughter, imagining she was ill, and that they were endeavoring to hide it from her.

When Zoe saw her mother pass, her heart beat quickly, she ran after her, hoping she would be recognized, but a saucy spaniel who never quitted Madame Epernay's side, and not knowing his young mistress under her disguise, began to bark at her, and soon had all the dogs in the house in his wake. There was nothing left for Zoe but flight, and in a moment she had jumped through a window and was climbing the high and slippery roof.

They awaited the return of Rosalie with anxiety; but she, unable to find the little girl, did not come back.

Madame Epernay called her daughter in an imploring voice. "Come, my child," she cried; "I shall not scold you." Then she visited every room in the house, the court-yard, the garden; she questioned every one; she, ordinarily so sweet, became impatient and violent through the excess of her uneasiness; she scolded all the servants, sent them out to look for the child, and reproached the porter for not having detained her. Then she returned to her room and threw herself on the bed in an agony of grief.

As the day advanced, her sorrow changed

into horrible despair. She had sent to all her friends and relatives, to the police, and all through the neighborhood, but no one had heard news of Zoe. All at once the idea occurred to her that Zoe had been killed by some frightful accident, and then she redoubled her tears; then she believed that the little girl was hiding somewhere and she would exclaim, " My child, my child, tell me the truth what has become of you ! Do not hide from me any longer. I shall not scold you, my dear little girl."

Zoe was still more to be pitied, for she heard her mother's cries, and was unable to answer, " I am here." In the excess of her sorrow, she imagined that the sorcerer might restore her to her primitive form, but he had disappeared, and left no trace behind him. So she remained all night in the passage-way facing the windows of her mother's apartment, not daring to enter through fear of the vigilant spaniel who lay on the rug near the door. She thought of writing to her mother, but she had neither pen, ink, nor paper, and even if she had, who would read, or reading believe, " My dear mamma, do not cry, I am a cat."

CHAPTER VI.

THE LETTER.

S soon as the day dawned, Zoe, fearing to re-enter the house, where she would have, at least, the sad satisfaction of being near her mother, climbed to the roof once more, where she might see without being seen. As she sat sad and quiet, she heard the noise of an opening window in the neighboring house, and, looking downward saw the interior of a pretty room. Books were scattered here and there on the different tables. Flowers stood in a pretty vase on the mantel, and a writing desk, small and compact, lay on the little table near the window. This attracted Zoe, who thought of the letter she wished to write, and she resolved to enter the apartment. She sprang to the window sill, and seeing no one near, bravely entered the room. The disturbance caused a piece of bread, lying on an easel near the door, to fall on the floor. Zoe eagerly seized it, black and dirty though it was from having been used to erase pencil marks from the picture in process of completion; but she had had nothing to eat since evening, and it soon disappeared.

After this splendid repast she prepared to write her letter; but the difficulty lay in tracing characters that would be legible.

After having made several curious lines, Zoe endeavored to read them, but alas! she could not. Zigzags and blots there were in plenty, profiles of noses, and scratches, but no letters — it was just what any cat would have written, nothing more. Impatient at seeing that she could accomplish nothing, she threw away her pen, and dipped her paw in the inkstand, trying to write with her nails; but this was another failure; the characters were more illegible than before.

She had already filled with ink all the papers on the table, the fauteuil, and on two or three books, when the occupant of the room entered.' This was a young girl, of about sixteen years, who seemed surprised to find a large cat which she had never before seen, writing at her desk.

Far from being displeased, Eglantine (the young lady was so called) appeared charmed to see so wise a cat, and covered Zoe with caresses, giving her bon-bons and milk, and the poor child under her strange guise was very grateful.

Zoe also remembered the words of the sorcerer, which in her first despair she had forgotten. "Thou shalt never recover thy own shape until some one shall say, "Zoe, I pardon thee!"—and then, the poor cat, so well treated, took courage, and began to hope that she would one day hear Eglantine, whom she had already begun to love, pronounce the words, "Zoe, I pardon thee."

CHAPTER VII.

TRIALS.

IN the evening, Zoe returned to her mother's house to hear the news, but Madame Epernay had gone away. The physicians, fearful of her reason, had ordered her departure from the scene of such cruel memories, and had advised a voyage to Italy, lest she should succumb to the force of her grief.

Zoe was very sad at the absence of her mother, and the deprivation of even seeing her at a distance threw her into profound melancholy. She knew that her mother would long remain inconsolable; but the idea that those surrounding her would endeavor to efface the memory of her child, tormented her. Zoe passed the night in the court-yard. It was very cold; the stable would have been much warmer, but she was afraid of the horses.

As soon as Eglantine re-opened the window of her room, Zoe returned to her. The young girl received her even more joyfully than on the preceding day, for she was now an old friend.

"Minette," said she, "come here." Zoe did not wish to be called by this name, and seemed unhappy because it had been given to her.

"Mignonne," said Eglantine, but Zoe did not stir.

"I must give you a name, pussie," said Eglantine, "since you are going to be mine, and you cannot tell me what your name is."

At these words, a bright idea entered Zoe's brain. She jumped at a bound through the window, ran over the roofs till she came to her own dwelling, and gliding through the halls, came at last to the door of her room. Everything was in disorder; playthings and dresses lay promiscuously on the floor, and for a moment she seemed at a loss. A pile of her little handkerchiefs lay on the bureau; she seized one adroitly in her mouth, and ran swiftly away. Zoe had embroidered her name in one of the corners, and returning to Eglantine, she showed her with her paw the three letters which composed it. " Zoe," said Eglantine aloud, and the cat jumped on her knees, thinking thereby to fix her attention.

In vain did her young mistress essay to call her by other names; the cat persisted in showing her the embroidery on the handkerchief; and Eglantine, seeing she wished to be called Zoe, supposed some one had given this name to her, and made up her mind to let her keep it.

Usually it is the mistress who educates the cat; but here it was the cat telling the mistress what she wished to be called. This seemed very singular; but Eglantine knew that domestic animals are intelligent, and was not greatly astonished.

Thus was Zoe established in the house with her own veritable name ; the greatest difficulty was over ; all she thought of now was to make some one say, ''I pardon you,' and the least little fault might render this possible.

But to obtain the pardon of her mistress it was necessary first to vex her, and that was not so easily managed, all at once.

Some one had given Eglantine a large box of bon-bons ; Zoe saw it, and made haste to eat all it contained, and joyously awaited the return of her mistress hoping that she would scold her severely.

But her hope was short lived ; Eglantine was no *gourmande*. She saw that Zoe had eaten the bonbons, and instead of being angry, she said, —

'' That was right, Zoe ; you knew I was saving them for you.''

Zoe was disappointed by this amiability, and she resolved to adopt some other plan.

Eglantine designed beautifully. For several days she had been working at a landscape, which she wished to show to her father. The picture was nearly finished; it needed but a few touches of the pencil to be entirely completed. Zoe, seeing that her mistress was much interested in the drawing, thought that if she should destroy it, Eglantine would be very angry. Consequently, one day when the young lady had gone out, Zoe pulled it from the easel, tore it in pieces, and covered the fragments with pencil marks, so as to destroy all vestige of the houses, trees and flowers that had made it so pretty a picture.

After this fine feat, she hid under the table, there to await the anger of her mistress.

Eglantine returned a few moments after, when she saw the floor strewn with bits of paper. She picked up a fragment, only to learn that her picture had been torn into pieces. But instead of flying into a fury, as Zoe had expected, she began to laugh.

"If my father saw this," she said, "how he would tease me! 'It serves you right,' he would say, 'for keeping cats around you.'"

With these words she threw the pieces into

the fire, and immediately set to work to begin another picture. Meanwhile, Zoe came bravely from her hiding-place, expecting first to receive a scolding, and then to hear, " Zoe, I pardon you ;" but Eglantine did not scold.

" Hide yourself quickly, Zoe," she said laughingly ; " my father is coming, and he does not like cats. And Zoe took herself away, sad and discouraged.

CHAPTER VIII.

ANOTHER TRIAL.

SEVERAL days after, hope returned to
her heart. Entering Eglantine's room,
Zoe perceived a beautiful wreath of roses that
had just been brought there. The maid had
been imprudent enough to lay them on the
foot of the bed, while the hair-dresser arranged Eglantine's braids, and she, seated at
her toilet, could not see what passed behind
her. Zoe saw that the moment was favorable; her mistress was going to a grand ball,
and the wreath of roses was a very important
affair; therefore it was necessary to destroy
it without hesitation. If Eglantine had endured patiently the loss of the bon-bons, and
the destruction of her picture, she could not

suffer the immolation of her garland. While the hair-dresser chatted volubly about the various *coiffures* he had arranged that day, Zoe stretched herself upon the flowers in such a manner that not a rose was left with out being crushed and broken. When the hair-dresser turned to place the wreath on Eglantine's head, what was his horror to find it utterly spoiled and useless.

"Miss Eglantine," he exclaimed; "see what this miserable cat has done! It will be impossible for you to wear these flowers;" and he held them up to her view.

Eglantine was not vain; she was right, she was so beautiful. The sight of the poor flowers instead of angering her made her laugh.

"I see that I shall have to be contented without a wreath to-day," she answered. "Fannie give me that spray of lilacs I wore the other day; all flowers look equally well with a white crape dress. Pussy you are fond of roses it seems."

At these words, Zoe ran out of the room

in a state of despair.   She was irritated beyond her patience.   "What!" thought she,
"not a spark of vanity! At the destruction
of her wreath, which would have vexed any
other lady, she is not a particle ill-humored."

Zoe reproached Eglantine for her sweetness as though it had been a crime; she
accused her of carelessness; she could not
pardon a good disposition which deranged
all her projects, destroyed all her hopes.
Thus do we often, among our friends, take a
good quality for a fault, because it annoys us.

CHAPTER IX.

RESENTMENT.

ZOE passed a month in sadness and discouragement. She was distressed at being a cat, and at not seeing her mother; she imagined that Madame Epernay had adopted one of her cousins, and this thought caused her to weep with jealousy. She despaired of vexing her mistress, and could not decide on any means by which to excite her displeasure. She wished to return to her original form, but, at the same time, she did not like to be ungrateful by offending Eglantine in any serious matter.

Eglantine had a little brother, into whose room the cat was never allowed to enter.

The boy was afraid of cats, and the servants had been forbidden to permit them to approach him. Notwithstanding their vigilance Zoe found means to introduce herself into the room, and jumping into the cradle, gave the child, in play, a blow with her paw.

But now something happened which she had not foreseen. She had scratched the child, involuntarily, and his eyelid began to bleed, while he cried out most piteously for help. Eglantine ran into the room. Oh, this time she was angry! She pushed Zoe away with great indignation, and the cat saw that she was not likely soon to be pardoned for having shown such cruelty.

After this circumstance Zoe did not dare to return to her mistress. She lived on the roof, and passed entire nights in complaining. She saw no chance of being restored to Eglantine's good graces. She knew that her little brother was always sick; that his eye was not healed; and, above all, she knew that Eglantine loved her no longer.

One night, sadder than ever, she was

seated on a gutter reflecting on the cruelty
of her fate ; all at once she saw a bright light
in the little boy's room. A lamp near the
bed had ignited the curtains ; every one was
at dinner, and no one knew of the danger.

Zoe saw the peril ; she rushed to the window, breaking a pane at the risk of cutting
her feet, and then seizing a little bell from
the table, she rang it so loudly that in an
instant all the servants were on the spot.
Eglantine was in the room as soon as they ;
she threw herself into the flames, and lifted
her little brother in her arms, in her emotion
manifesting no astonishment at seeing a cat
ringing a bell. The servants were not so
indifferent. They speedily extinguished the
fire ; then the danger past, and the poor
child reassured, they burst forth into excla-
mations of wonder at the manner in which
he had been saved.

Eglantine, hearing their enthusiasm, rushed
to thank the cat which had saved her brother's life.

But Zoe, who feared the resentment of

her mistress, dared not to approach her, and as soon as the child was out of danger, she climbed back to her gutter. However, she did not remain there long, for she heard her name called on all sides. " Zoe, Zoe," said Eglantine in a sweet and beseeching voice, and Zoe slowly descended from the gutter, looking about her as she advanced. Timidly she entered her mistress's apartment. "Come here, Zoe," said Eglantine, smiling, and reaching out her hand ; but Zoe ran to hide under the table.

" I am not angry with you, my pretty little cat," said Eglantine. " If you did scratch Frederic the other day, you have saved his life to-night ; come here, do not hide yourself."

But Zoe did not venture from her retreat ; she waited, she hoped for the magic words that would put an end to her troubles.

Then, Eglantine, becoming more importunate, approached the table. " Come, then, little one," she said, in a caressing voice,

" do not be afraid of a scolding; I am not angry ; *Zoe, I pardon you.*"

She had hardly pronounced these words when the prediction of the sorcerer was accomplished ; Zoe resumed her proper shape ; she was a little girl again.

CHAPTER X.

THE RESTORATION.

YOU may imagine Eglantine's surprise at seeing a pretty little girl under the table, instead of the great ugly cat, to which she had been speaking. Zoe threw herself into her arms.

"Take me back to my mother!" she exclaimed, "she will be so glad to see me."

Eglantine, who was a very sensible girl, comprehended immediately Zoe's desire to be restored to her mother; but she wished, before taking her home, to prepare Madame Epernay; fearing that after so great a sorrow, the sudden joy might be fatal to her.

Madame Epernay had returned to Paris a few days previous.

This good mother was very ill; six months had elapsed since the loss of her child, and she had never ceased to weep for her. Zoe was impatient to return to her, and it required all the art in the world to hinder her from running to embrace her. She could not believe that the pleasure of finding her little girl might be dangerous to her; children never see any danger in happiness.

Eglantine, pitying her impatience, went in person to Madame Epernay, inventing some fable to herself with which to prepare the mind of the unhappy mother for this great joy.

" Madame," said she, timidly approaching the lady, whom she found in tears, and surrounded by objects which recalled her child, " pardon me, if I awake in your heart a sorrowful and bitter memory."

" Speak, madamoiselle, if it is of Zoe, do not fear to sadden me further by talking of her — for I think of her always."

" Have you never heard anything of her

since the day she so mysteriously disappeared? Have you no hope?"

" Alas!" responded the weeping mother. " Alas! No. But your eyes sparkle, do not deceive me — oh! have you heard — do you know — can you tell me anything?"

"I may be mistaken," continued Eglantine, composing as she went along, her charitable fable; " I have heard mention made of a child of the same age as yours, who was stolen by gypsies six months ago."

" My poor Zoe! it is she, she is living!" cried Madame Epernay in a delirium of hope.

" It may be that it is not she!" Eglantine replied; " I have not seen the child of whom I speak, but I can see it, and I am not sure that it is yours; but, madame, if you will lend or show me a portrait of your little girl, I may be able."

"There is her portrait!" interrupted Madame Epernay; " it resembles her, although not nearly so pretty as my little Zoe." With these words she detached a locket from her watch chain, and gave it to Eglantine. "Oh, my God!" she cried, "if I could but find her."

Eglantine took her departure, promising to return in a few hours. That evening about nine o'clock, Madame Epernay saw Eglantine tripping through the corridor to her apartment. The young girl appeared so joyous that the lady was prepared for good news.

"I have great hope, madame," said Eglantine; "I have not seen the child, but my maid, who told me the story, has; she is fair, very fair, and about eight years of age."

"So is my daughter."

"She is named Aglae, or Zoe; my maid does not remember which; but she remarked that the child had large blue eyes, with long brown lashes, and very light curls."

"It is she; it is she; oh, where can I see her?"

"Be careful, madame; the gypsies will instantly leave Paris if they hear we suspect them; to-morrow"—

"To-morrow — to-morrow! I cannot wait till to-morrow. Bring her to me; let me go to her. She is mine; she is mine!"

Eglantine had not the courage to pursue the deception further; this joy, this impatience made her tremble.

"Speak," cried Madame Epernay; "why may I not see her to-day?"

"Because you are too weak for so much joy," replied Eglantine.

"No, no!" exclaimed the poor mother, "happiness gives me strength; I can see my child without weeping. Bring her to me, bring her to me!"

They heard a noise in the adjoining chamber.

"I see," cried Madame Epernay. "It is she! You have brought her! Zoe! Zoe! my child! my child!"

"Mamma," replied a dear familiar voice, "it is I; I am coming."

And Zoe lay weeping upon her mother's bosom.

CHAPTER XI.

NOT A DREAM.

"ZOE, Zoe;" cried Rosalie, opening the shutters to admit the morning sun, which streamed in brightly on the little bed, with its pretty blue silk covers and lace pillows. "Zoe, get up quickly; it is eight o'clock, and your cousins are here. Mamma will be dressed in a little while, and what will she think if her little girl is not ready to congratulate her on her birthday morning."

Zoe moved uneasily on her pillow, but made no effort to rise.

"What! you are not getting up," continued Rosalie, moving about the chamber as she spoke. "I called you at five, as you bade me, and the early awaking made you cross, I suppose, for you scolded me about your lilac dress, and fell asleep again while I was ironing it. Here it is now, fresh and pretty as ever, and here are your new pink ribbons."

Zoe sat up in bed and rubbed her eyes. "Is that you, Rosalie," she said wonderingly. "You did not run away, then?"

"Run away! No. Why should I run away? And on your dear mamma's birthday. You are not awake yet."

"Is it mamma's birthday, Rosalie? Are you not joking?"

"Joking? Is the child crazy? You have slept your senses away. To be sure I am not joking. Anna and Delphine are here with their pretty presents — and see your lilac dress at the foot of the bed."

"And — and — I have not been a cat," said Zoe, timidly, looking about her, and seeing that everything was familiar and unchanged.

"A cat!" exclaimed Rosalie. "Mon Dieu! the child is dreaming," and very much alarmed, she lifted the little girl in her arms, and stood her upon a stool in front of the mirror.

"Truly you have not been a cat, and you are not a cat now. Look at yourself, you are my own little Zoe, and you are going to be dressed immediately."

But Zoe shook her head, and went to the window overlooking the court-yard. From a tall, narrow chimney opposite she saw smoke rising in thick volumes.

"What place is that, Rosalie?" she asked, gravely.

"That is where old Mainton, the chemist lives."

"Does chemist mean sorcerer, Rosalie? And do chemists change little girls into cats?"

Rosalie burst into a fit of laughter. "I see it now," she said. "You have been dreaming. Do you not remember, last night, after I had put out the light and tucked you in, as I sat near the window, I said that chimney made me think of a magazine furnace, and the old man Mainton reminded me of a sorcerer?".

"And I asked you to tell me something about sorcerers," said Zoe, eagerly.

"Yes, and I did a very foolish thing when I told you the story of 'Hadziun a Poun.' It gave you a bad dream."

Zoe heaved a deep sigh.

"And so I have not been a cat, — I dreamed it, I suppose. And Eglantine,—do you know a young lady called Eglantine, who lives just over there?" pointing with her finger in the direction of a tall, handsome house, whose courtyard met their own.

"That is a dream, too, madamoiselle. Madame de La Motte lives there, all alone, with her cats and dogs. She is a very old lady. There is no one called Eglantine in that house."

Zoe was silent for a few moments. Slowly her thoughts shaped themselves into the truth. She had fallen asleep during the recital of Rosalie's story of a sorcerer, and had dreamed of the magician all night. Awakened very early as she had been, she had gone to sleep again when Rosalie left the room to iron her dress. And then she had dreamed that terrible dream.

Suddenly she threw her arms around Rosalie's neck.

"Oh, Rosalie, Rosalie!" she cried with tears in her eyes and in her voice. "I will never be naughty again, never. Quick, take me to mamma, I feel so strange I cannot see her soon enough."

Madame Epernay could not understand the unusual warmth of her little girl's caresses that morning, for she was always very affectionate — neither could she comprehend why she never left her side that day, but followed her like one who fears to lose a treasure. But that night, seated beside her bed, while she recited the history of her strange dream, the fond mother did not wonder at the redoubled affection that had shown its ardor after such a terrible experience; and the brown lashes had long closed over Zoe's blue eyes before she pressed her last kiss on the pure white forehead, and left her to her guardian angel.

A WHOLESOME LESSON.

CHAPTER I.

THE CHILDREN'S PARTY.

ALICE Morris was a little girl, with many good qualities; but she had a fault that had grown to be so common, and made her at times so disagreeable, that one could not listen to her without impatience. She was so given to exaggeration, that to hear her tell a story, was enough to cause laughter and derision. She lived in New York, and, as an instance of her exaggeration, she would say : " I could go from here to New Orleans without sleeping."   Or, " It is almost thirteen thousand miles from here to New Orleans."

" To-morrow morning," she would announce, " I shall get up very early, and write twelve French verbs before breakfast."

Her father, tired and ashamed of this ridiculous fault, resolved to correct her. One day she exclaimed in her ordinary manner: " Oh! I love dancing; I could dance three days and three nights without stopping, and without being in the least tired." Her father, wishing to take her at her word, gave orders that preparation should be made for a grand party.

Alice, enchanted with this prospect, passed the days which preceded it in practising her steps that she might be in complete readiness when the time came. The day soon arrived.

At noon, her maid came into her room, bringing an elegant costume which she told Alice her mother desired her to wear, and

begged her to make haste and be dressed, as
the musicians had arrived, and the ball was
about to begin. Alice would not believe
this, and ran to her father to obtain an explanation.

"Is it true, papa, that the party is going
to begin in the middle of the day?" she
asked.

"Yes, my child," Mr. Morris replied;
"the ladies have desired that the ball commence early on account of their children,
who are not allowed to sit up late; but since
you are so fond of dancing, my little girl,
you may remain all night, if it will amuse
you."

Alice thought this very reasonable, and
thanking her father for his permission, went
back to her room, and was soon ready for
the festivities of the day. All the shutters
were closed and the lamps lighted, and it
was only here and there that a ray of sun-
light penetrated through some chink or
crevice. The parlor was soon filled with
gaily dressed children, and Alice, in her

character of hostess, was the gayest and liveliest of all. She lost no time standing still
or sitting down, I assure you; never was
little girl more restless. Her father looked
at her from time to time, and smiled to think
how it would all end.

The children frolicked and gambolled until
eight in the evening; then supper was announced, and they pressed eagerly forward
to the dining-room. They had well earned
the repast, they were about to enjoy, by the
length and excitement of their exercise.

Alice, who had been the leader of every
game, was very hungry, and advanced to the
table with the children, with the intention
of doing the honors, it is true, but also
with the desire and expectation of getting
something to eat.

Just as she was seating herself, her father
placed his hand on her shoulder.

"The grand ball is about to commence,
my dear; the dancing will begin immediately; it is not worth while to remain here with
the children, particularly as you are so fond

of dancing; come, take your place in the quadrille, and let us see how you have profited by your lessons."

Alice heard this with emotions far from joyful, and bade a wistful adieu to the table loaded with delicacies, envying the little boys and girls that were filling their plates with cakes and dainties, and wishing that she could have even a cup of coffee before leaving the dining-room. But she was obliged to leave this tempting supper, and begin a new ball without having had time to rest from the first, without having been able to sit down for an instant. It seemed cruel to her; but she remembered having said she would like to dance three days and three nights without stopping, and this was not the end of the first, and Alice was too proud to cry "mercy."

CHAPTER II.

THE GRAND BALL.

N. entering the ball room she was charmed with the view before her. Hardly twelve years of age, she had never before attended a large party; here all was light, perfume and flowers. She was delighted, for the time being, and forgot her hunger in this new excitement.

All at once she began to feel a great contempt for her little companions, who were resting in the other room, compelled to sit quietly and eat cakes, like turbulent children, while she was enjoying the privilege of being in grown-up society. A few minutes ago she had been a gay, romping child;

now, all was changed, and she sat, sober and solemn, as became her new dignity.

She endeavored to assume an air of gravity, and to such an extent was she successful, that several persons thought she had been scolded. But Alice, quite unconscious of what was passing in their minds, preserved her stern exterior, in spite of their compassionate glances. She was not at all in bad humor; on the contrary, never before had she been so proud and happy.

It was quite another thing, when a young man, in full party costume and white gloves, approaching her with the greatest respect, uttered these wonderful words: "Miss, will you honor me with your hand for the first quadrille?" Alice was so flattered that she could scarcely reply. "Yes, sir; with pleasure."

With pleasure! that was the sincere truth. She was about to dance in earnest with a young man who wore gloves, a cavalier, who said: "Miss, will you honor me with your hand for the first quadrille," and not with a rough little boy, who would say, " Come on, cousin Alice, and dance with me." How rude that familiar invitation seemed to her now !

CHAPTER III.

THE QUADRILLE.

ALICE was so happy that she entirely forgot her fatigue. She danced gracefully, and soon had many offers. Dance succeeded dance, and after having been on her feet all day, she began to feel extremely tired ; but there was nothing left to her but to hold out as long as possible. The floor was very smooth and slippery, and her tired little feet were more than once on the point of playing her false.

"You love dancing, Miss Alice?" asked her partner.

"Yes, sir."

"And well you may, for you dance beautifully."

Alice put her feet close together to rest them a little, and her partner, observing the movement, said:

"The floor is quite slippery, particularly to one who is not accustomed to it; but you will soon be used to the smooth surface," and with these words, the quadrille being finished, he conducted her to her place.

Alice felt piqued at the unconscious young man. How could he know she was unaccustomed to dancing at balls. A few moments ago she had been all admiration, but now she thought him impertinent.

Another young man invited her to dance immediately, then another, and another, until she was obliged to reply to all, "I am engaged." Six quadrilles in perspective, when she had already danced twelve, for she had been tripping it since mid-day. It was almost too much. But then, her vanity would give her no peace, and her father was present. She had declared her ability to dance three days and nights without fatigue. Her next partner was not at all agreeable. A fat little man, with a red nose, and very short breath, he puffed and puffed, till the people in the vicinity wondered if he might not be on the verge of an apoplectic fit.

"You love dancing, miss?" he said, between the puffs, in a hoarse voice. Then, without waiting for an answer, he added: "I love it, too; but you do things too quickly here. In my country, that dear old Germany, they waltz very sweetly, and it is less fatiguing, I do assure you. I have only danced four quadrilles, and, I confess it, I am extremely tired."

These words reminded Alice that she, too, was fatigued; and her courage began to abandon her. Her next partner was a solemn young man, who marched up and down, as though he were the undertaker at a funeral, who seemed rather to be performing a duty than a pleasure, and who led her through the dance with an air of resignation. Still, he thought himself obliged to be polite to the young lady of the house, and he said to her, very gravely and slowly :

" Do you like dancing, miss ? "

" Yes," replied Alice, turning her head away as she did so. This prevented all further conversation.

The next, and the next, and the next, asked her the same question, till she began to ask herself why their conversation never varied. It was because they did not know what else to say to a little girl of twelve years. But Alice, in blissful ignorance, continued to preserve her dignified exterior.

CHAPTER IV.

THE THIRTEENTH QUADRILLE.

ALICE, disenchanted, was so disgusted with dancing that she thought she could never again like the amusement; she regretted her little cousins, and longed to be laughing at some of their fooleries.

Exhausted by fatigue, she was thinking of some pretext to retire, when a friend of her father, an old colonel, about sixty years of age, advanced towards her, and exclaimed:

"Here you are, my pretty little Alice; I must ask a favor of you; I must absolutely dance with you. My dear, I have not seen you for five years. Come, let us be quick, I hear the music, we have not a moment to lose."

Alice was obliged to follow him, but she was not quite so eager for the dance as he. The poor child did not wish to disoblige her father's friend, one who had been very kind and generous towards her since her earliest childhood. So she summoned courage to dance once more.

But this dance was destined to be a trial; the old man went through it with all his heart, and gave Alice an extra turn at every figure. He looked so large and comical in his green gloves and blue spectacles, that the attention of the company was fixed on him, while Alice, who by contrast, looked smaller and more fragile than she really was, could not help feeling her cherished dignity slowly vanishing.

Her father, who stood near, took pity on her. "It is long past your bed-time, my dear," said he; "I am afraid you are greatly fatigued."

But Alice, who saw the involuntary smile on his face as he spoke, answered promptly: "I, papa? No, indeed; I intend to dance all night."

And Mr. Morris, hoping to give her some rest, in spite of herself, requested the musicians to play a waltz. Alice could not waltz, and looked about her for a place where she might rest unobserved. She hoped the dancers would forget her, and that those around her would soon take home their brothers and sisters, for several had already quitted the room. Alice saw them depart with envy.

"Oh, dear!" she thought, "they are going to bed and to sleep." Every time she bade adieu to a lady or gentleman, she prolonged her good-night with the hope that the dancers would forget her existence; but no, they were pitiless, they followed her even into the ante-room with their importunities.

The ceaseless music, joined to the fatigue which was overcoming her, began to be unendurable; everything seemed to turn round; she could scarcely see. Sleep weighed down her eyelids, she did not know where she was. This eternal dancing seemed like a terrible nightmare from which she was never to escape. She felt oppressed. These ever recurring words sounded like a condemnation in her ears :

"To your places." "English chain." "Balance to partners." "Forward two." "Right hand across." "Left hand back." "All hands around."

She sought refuge on a lounge that stood near the entrance of a pretty little boudoir at the end of the parlors. But she was speedily interrupted in her half slumber by these terrible words :

" Miss Alice, I have found a *vis-a-vis*, we can dance this set. The quadrille is about to commence," and then began the odious refrain :

" To your places." "English chain." " Balance to partners." " Forward two." " Right hand across." " Left hand back." " All hands round."

After this was finished, Alice went in search of her father and mother, who were playing whist with some friends in the library. As she approached them, she assumed a joyous air.

"Are you enjoying your game?" she inquired, smiling.

"Yes, my child," said her mother; "but how is it that you are not sleepy?"

"Oh, it is because I am amusing myself so well."

Then a partner came to claim her, and the refrain was repeated:

"To your places." "English chain." "Balance to partners." "Forward two." "Right hand across." "Left hand back." "All hands round." The last words were welcome, for they at least meant a little rest.

CHAPTER V.

SLIGHTLY FATIGUED.

IT was four o'clock in the morning; it was spring; the day began to break. A window was open, facing the street, in one of the grand parlors already deserted. Alice sat on a fauteuil in front of the window, gazing sadly into the street.

"It was daylight when the children's party began," she thought; "the night is past, the day has returned, and I must still dance." For you see she did not forget her foolish assertion, and she thought herself very silly for having made it. However, seeing that the ball was nearly over, she wished still farther to prove her courage, and resolved to be brave until every one had gone. "When the musicians have left," she thought, "there can be no more opportunity to dance."

Ah! what forces you to dance, little simpleton, but your pride and obstinacy?

That is what I should have replied, had I been there; but it happened that I was not invited to the ball.

At this juncture, several milkmen passed in their waggons, and were annoyed at the carriages that blocked the way. " What need is there of sitting up so late and inconveniencing poor folks," said they.

" And can they not amuse themselves without obstructing the road?"

Alice heard the remark. "As though this was amusement," she thought. The fresh morning air penetrated her senses, and filled her with such a soothing influence that the music seemed to her a distant strain, which grew fainter and fainter every moment. The fatal words fell on her ear as before, but not unpleasantly. She had knelt on the bench with her arms on the stone balustrade, that she might look down into the street; insensibly her head drooped, and fell upon her hands; Alice was asleep. The gradual movement had disarranged her hair, the comb that confined it fell to the pavement, and only one little flower remained to tell of glories departed. The young man who was to have been her partner sought her in vain; she was hidden by the window shutters, which had closed behind her. Her father, not seeing her, thought she had gone to bed at last, and her mother was of the same opinion. Her slumber was so profound that she did not feel the cold, nor hear the noise of the street, which increased every moment. Perhaps she might have remained there till evening, if a policeman had not noticed a comb on the pavement with some teeth broken out, and a little spray of artificial flowers, which seemed to have been there but a short time.

A natural curiosity caused him to raise his eyes to the balcony above, to the window from which these objects appeared to have fallen. Then he perceived several long curls drooping over the balustrade.

Dismayed at this sight, he recoiled several paces, and saw Alice asleep on the window sill. As she did not move, and her hair was dishevelled, he concluded that she was dead, that she had been murdered. For this was a young and romantic policeman, with a taste for the melodramatic, and fond of reading sensational newspapers.

He knocked at the door, and awakened a footman who was sleeping in the hall. The footman called the housemaid, who was also asleep on a lounge.

" A dreadful thing has occurred in your house," said the policeman; but the house-maid stretched out her arms with a yawn, not understanding what he said.

" A great misfortune has happened," re-peated the policeman, " a murder," he added, for greater effect.

" A murder !" repeated footman and house-maid in concert.

" Yes, a murder ! A young lady has been

assassinated during the *fete*." (This was a melodramatic phrase, and he thought it well put in.)

"Ah, *mon Dieu!* It must be Miss Alice," said the young lady's maid, who now appeared from some other corner of the corridor.

"I have been waiting for her all night in her room, and she never came." Then she ran with wide-open eyes to Mr. Morris.

"Oh, sir," she exclaimed, "a dreadful thing has happened Miss Alice."

"My daughter," said Mr. Morris, uneasily.

"Yes, sir; a man saw her in a fainting-fit by a window." "I said fainting-fit so as not to frighten him," she explained to the people who gave egress to Mr. Morris through their midst. "But it is far worse — she has been murdered."

At these words every one crowded to the windows — the music ceased, the dancing was interrupted, and all the shutters of the various windows were opened in an instant.

"Here she is, here she is," cried one of the

young dancers who had *murdered* Alice, and they all hastened to his side.

"She is on her knees," said one.

"She is sound asleep," said another.

"She has fainted," said the chambermaid, endeavoring to revive her.

"Be quiet," said Mr. Morris; "let her sleep till to-morrow, if she will; she has need of repose, I assure you, and I am confident you can remove her from here without awaking her."

CHAPTER VI.

A WELL CHOSEN SARCASM.

AS it proved, they removed the little girl to her room, and undressed her without having disturbed her slumber.

That evening, at five o'clock, while the rest of the family awaited dinner in the saloon, her mother announced that Alice had just awakened.

Her father and cousins looked impatiently for her coming. When she appeared, she was greeted with laughter, and Alice, greatly mortified, began to cry.

"Come, my child," said her father; "do not cry. I am certain you are quite cured."

"Oh, yes, yes, papa," said Alice, weeping

bitterly, " I will never dance again as long as I live."

" Take care," replied her father, " that is an exaggeration also ; do not forswear dancing altogether ; I am sure you will like it better than ever, in the course of time."

" Alice," said a mischievous cousin, " won't you come to Mrs. Volnar's party this evening? They say it will be charming."

" Naughty girl," replied Alice, half laughing, half crying, " you know well that I cannot even walk."

" Come, children," said her father, " do not torment her ; let us think no more about the affair ; and I am sure Alice will never again give us cause to remember it by a similar fault."

They changed the conversation ; but the mischievous little cousin, seating herself at the piano, began playing the well-known air " *Danse n'est pas ce que j'aime*," which may be translated into, " I do not love dancing," or " dancing is not what I love."

All the family laughed at this incident, which was just to the point. It was adopted as an expression, and whenever Alice was tempted to indulge in her old exaggerations, her father would playfully hum the old air, and it was enough to recall her.

Let this story teach you, my little readers, how great is the fault of exaggeration, and that the only means of curing persons addicted to it is by forcing them to keep their promises.

THE YOUNG BALLAD SINGER.

ON a winter's day in the year 1799, a woman of about thirty-five years of age, of distinguished appearance, but poorly attired, traversed the Rue St. Denis, looking at all the houses where bills for apartments were displayed, as if in search of a lodging. She leaned on the arm of a young person, who might, perhaps, have seen sixteen or seventeen years, and whose pretty figure, and sweet and noble features attracted the notice of the passers-by, in spite of the common stuff dress and faded hat which she wore. On the other side the lady held by the hand a little girl of six years old, fresh and smiling, and whose cheerful babble at times dissipated even the melancholy imprinted on the features of her two companions.

These three persons stopped at last at the entrance of a passage, which led to a house of poor appearance, but yet neat and clean. Here she ascended to the fourth floor, which consisted of two bed-rooms and a little sitting-room, and these she hired at a rent of fifty francs per month.

She who was lodged in so modest a habitation was born, and for a long time had lived, in opulence. She was the widow of the Marquis de Rostain, whom she accompanied abroad in 1792; and her property, like that of her husband, had become the property of the nation. The marquis had died at Frankfort during the preceding year, leaving his wife and two children with only two hundred louis d'ors, the poor remains of a considerable sum which he had when he left France. Such means were evidently quite insufficient to enable the marchioness and her daughters to reside in a foreign city, where, without relations or friends to aid them, she could not even hope to reap any benefits from her talents and industry.

Alarmed by the unpromising prospects of her childern, she did not hesitate for their sakes to brave everything, in the hope of releasing them from poverty. So soon, therefore, as time had somewhat soothed the first excess of her grief for the loss of her husband, she set out for France, where she had formerly been condemned to the scaffold, and where she only ventured to return under the assumed name of Madame Dupré.

The Marchioness de Rostain had a cousin-german in Paris, who, though a great deal older than she, had formerly loved her as a sister. The Count de Sannois had not emi-grated, and his son had entered the French army at a very early age, where he became so much distinguished for his bravery, that he was rapidly promoted to the highest honors.   As more than once Madame de Rostain had seen the name of her young relation mentioned with praise in the journals, it was especially upon the protection of Monsieur de Sannois that she reckoned as a means for recovering, if possible, a part of her fortune, or, at least, to secure the erasure of her name from the fatal list.

What, then, was her disappointment when, on arriving in Paris, she learned that M. de Sannois had been travelling in Italy for six months; that the period of his return was uncertain, though it was supposed that it would be soon; and that his son was in Egypt, where he had followed Napoleon.

Madame de Rostain, who had not now remaining more than half of the small sum left to her by her husband, would have given herself up to despair, if her courage had not been supported by that of her eldest daughter.

Though Leontine was scarcely sixteen years old, her character and intelligence, developed by misfortune, were far beyond her years. She consoled her mother, and reminded her of the time when, in order to support the expenses of the long illness which finally deprived them of Monsieur de Rostain, they had both united in their efforts of industry.

"Why cannot we do in Paris what we did at Frankfort, mamma?" said the amiable girl. "Since it is so important that you should not be recognized by any one, and it is necessary we should live in the greatest solitude, we can lodge cheaply in one of those quarters not frequented by the fashionable world, and only go out of an evening to take the air, while we work during the day. It will be easy for you to dispose of our work to some shopkeeper, who will only know you under the name of Madame Dupré, and the money we can thus obtain, joined to what we have still left, will keep us very well till the return of our cousin."

Madame de Rostain resolved to follow the advice of Leontine, and did not delay therefore in establishing herself in the humble apartments of which we have spoken; not, however, without shedding many a tear over the fate of her poor children. For a small monthly payment, an old woman who lodged in the same house, came every morning to relieve them of the rougher part of the household duties, and Leontine undertook all the rest. She seemed to have more than one pair of hands, for she would not suffer her mother to do anything; and as soon as she found that their food, purchased at the shop of an indifferent cook, did not suit the delicate appetite of Madame de Rostain, she learned herself to prepare the frugal meals of the family. With what tenderness, with what love, the poor mother followed with her eyes that charming creature, always calm, always smiling, who seemed even to take pleasure in the most painful and fatiguing duties!

So as soon as Leontine had finished what she called her work, she would come gaily and sit down beside her mother and sister, and go on with her embroidery, or make a purse, a reticule, or some other of those fancy articles for which Madame de Rostain had found a sale at the shop of a great mercer in the Rue St. Denis, and who paid for them a very small, but ready-money price.

Madame de Rostain herself, and even the little Juliet, never quitted the needle during the day; and when the evening came, it was a great relief for the whole family to go and take a long walk upon the boulevards, whenever the weather would permit.

One evening the mother and daughters had been as far as the Madeleine, and were coming back very much fatigued, when they were stopped just by the Rue St. Denis, not only by a number of persons who had collected there, but by the attractive sounds of a very beautiful voice which was heard from the midst of the crowd.

A woman whose face was concealed under a black veil, was singing, to her own accompaniment on the guitar, a very difficult Italian air; and she sung, too, with much more taste and musical knowledge than could have been expected from an artist of that class.

As soon as she had finished, the bystanders eagerly threw their pieces of money into the little basket which was placed at her feet.

"That woman's singing is quite surprising," said Leontine; "allow me, mamma, to give her this little bit of money."

Then with the consent of her mother she threw six sous into the basket.

The music which they had heard formed the subject of conversation with Madame de Rostain and her daughters till the time of going to bed; and the next morning Leontine's mind was so much occupied by it, that she asked the charwoman whether that poor creature who sung so well was known in the neighborhood.

"Ah, have you heard her?" answered Mother Boudreau; "has she not a charming throat? It is like that of a nightingale. Ah, I could live well for a week out of her profits for one evening!"

"Do you believe, then," said Leontine,

"that if that poor unfortunate could make any savings, she would continue such a melancholy trade?"

"Bah, bah!" said the old woman, "she has no economy; she spends; she drinks!"

"Do you know her, then?" said Mademoiselle de Rostain.

"Not at all," answered the woman. "It is not more than six weeks that she has come every Thursday evening to sing on our boulevard; she does not belong to the quarter; she is some street-walker, no doubt."

Leontine did not think so ill of her, and could not endure to hear her slandered; besides that, the talent of the poor woman had captivated her. She therefore immediately broke off the conversation, which had by no means diminished her pity for the singer.

Before their establishment at Frankfort, M. de Rostain and his family had spent two years in Italy; and Leontine, whose voice was superb, had taken lessons of the best masters in that country, and thereby greatly improved her natural taste for music. Thus, when sitting by her mother at work, she was incessantly singing snatches of the airs which she had formerly practised, and on the day alluded to she repeated with an accuracy, that was truly remarkable, the song which the poor woman had sung on the preceding evening.

"What a pity it is, Leontine," said little Juliet, when her sister had finished the air, ".that you have not your piano to accompany you!"

"Or at least a guitar," answered Leontine; "that Italian music does not do well without an accompaniment." It was the first time that Leontine had expressed any thing approaching to a regret relative to the amusements of her past life; and as Madame de Rostain was by no means indifferent upon the subject, two days afterwards, when, according to her custom, she carried home the week's work, she brought back with her for her beloved daughter a very beautiful guitar which she had bought.

"Oh, mamma!" exclaimed Leontine, as she covered her mother's hand with kisses, "I blame myself for having mentioned the guitar; you have been spending a great deal of money for me, I am sure."

"No, not much, my love," answered the poor mother; "and at any rate we shall now be able to have some music, which will be a great enjoyment for me, Leontine."

Every evening, indeed, after the guitar was bought, Leontine, before going to bed, took her guitar, and sung the airs which were the greatest favorites with her mother and sister, and this innocent amusement made a pleasant termination to their sad and toilsome days.

The summer, however, had quite passed away without any change in the position of the little family. Monsieur de Sannois had not yet returned, and the people at his hotel were even ignorant in what part of Italy he then was. Meanwhile the incessant toil of

Madame de Rostain and her daughters was insufficient for their support, and the trifle of money in their possession diminished day by day.

Leontine, who denied herself almost every necessary, entreated Madame de Rostain not to renounce various little luxuries, which her age, and the long enjoyment of a large fortune, had converted into actual wants. Her supplications upon this point were the more earnest, because she perceived the health of her beloved mother visibly declining. Madame de Rostain grew wretchedly thin; she became fatigued with the evening walk, which she was compelled to abridge from day to day; but in which she obstinately persisted, in order that her daughters might have the benefit of the air.

Very soon she could only take a turn upon the nearest boulevard, and sit down there to rest for an hour. Leontine had then plenty of time to observe the poor singer, and she soon found that the woman collected a great deal of money; for the passers-by were continually throwing small pieces of silver into her little basket.

Leontine began at last to think that Mother Boudreau was perhaps right, when on a sudden the singer's visits to the boulevard ceased; and more than a month having passed without her reappearing, Leontine pleased herself with the belief that the poor woman had acquired a little fortune.

The health of Madame de Rostain grew worse every day; at last she consented to consult a physician, who declared her to be seriously ill, and forbade her to pursue any kind of employment. The nervous weakness of her head rendered her incapable of managing any kind of business, and Leontine took charge of the ten louis, which were all that remained to supply their wants. The poor girl felicitated herself upon this arrangement; for the regimen ordered by the physician being somewhat expensive, Madame de Rostain would never have followed it, if her daughter had not been able to conceal from her the cost of the medicines, as well as of other contingent expenses.

To crown all these misfortunes, Leontine, who had not only to attend to the domestic arrangements, but also to nurse her mother, had no time left for her needlework, so that at last she could not count the money which remained in the purse without shedding tears. This sum would not last beyond the month, and Madame de Rostain, so far from becoming convalescent, was often unable to leave her bed; each hour as it passed brought them some new misery. Leontine carefully concealed her cruel anxieties from her mother and sister, and many a night, while Juliet slept peacefully beside her, she watered her pillow with her tears. With inexpressible anguish of heart she prayed to God to send them some assistance; but when day appeared she dried up her tears, in order to enter her mother's chamber with a serene countenance, and a smile upon her lips.

At last the fatal moment arrived. A few

sous alone remained in the purse; and Mother Boudreau for a week past had given credit for bread and meat. Madame de Rostain, then, must die for want of help, and Juliet must die of hunger.

"My God!" exclaimed Leontine, "to-morrow, to-morrow, perhaps, I shall be unable longer to hide from them our frightful position. I must tell them everything."

The poor girl had cleared the table of the frugal dinner, which Juliet alone had touched, and, seated beside her mother's bed, remained for some time plunged in the most dreadful thoughts. It was not light enough for her to see to work, nor dark enough for her to venture to light the only candle which remained in the house.

"It is a long time since you have touched your guitar, Leontine," said Madame de Rostain. "Sing me something; I should like to hear you."

Though far from being in a mood to sing, as may be well imagined, the poor girl would not refuse to her mother the only pleasure she could enjoy. She therefore obeyed, with a heart oppressed with grief, and eyes full of tears; and while her sweet and beautiful voice soothed the heart of Madame de Rostain, a sudden thought came into her mind; she remembered the singer of the boulevard. That woman had disappeared, and whoever could take her place would be likely to secure the same receipts. But it would be equivalent to asking alms! Alms! well, even that Leontine thought she was bound to do, in order to procure assistance for the beloved beings of whom she was now the sole support. Since Madame de Rostain had been confined to the house, Leontine had been compelled both to fetch and take home the work to the mercer in the Rue St. Denis; and she had always waited till night before she ventured upon this short journey into the street. The next evening, under the pretence of going to the shop, she said good-by to her mother, and bidding Juliet take care of her in her absence, she went back to her own room, put on a large black veil, and with her guitar in her hand, soon reached the boulevard.

The heart of the poor little girl beat so violently that she feared she would not be able to summon courage for the execution of her project. But she remembered her mother and Juliet, and placing a little basket on the ground, she began to sing the Italian romance of Nina, one of the tender compositions of Paesiello. During the first strain several persons stopped, and very soon a crowd had gathered round the young cantatrice, every one speaking in surprise and admiration. Leontine did not hear these praises; but the readiness which was shown in dropping contributions into her little basket, informed her of her success. By the time the first couplet was finished, the audience had contributed according to their means, and Leontine judged that the receipts must be considerable. She therefore sung the second couplet, rather as an acknowledgment of the benevolence of her auditors, than with the expectation of obtaining more. One young man, however, approached just as she was concluding, and threw in his offering, saying something at the same time, the import of which she could not catch.

As soon as Leontine reached home, she hastened to count her treasure, and her surprise was only equalled by her joy, when, among the pence and the silver, she discovered a piece of gold.

"Twenty francs!" she exclaimed; " twenty francs and fifteen make thirty-five. Here is more than enough for the week's expenses. Next Thursday I will go and sing there again; I will sing every Thursday till she gets well. Oh, my God!" she added, clasping her hands, "I render thee thanks for having inspired me with that thought." The following Thursday, therefore, in pursuance of her resolution, Leontine revisited the boulevard. As soon as she had reached the spot she had chosen, she began to play the prelude of a little Italian air.

"'The Romance of Nina!'" cried a soft voice near her.

" Let them have what they like," thought the poor child, to whom the music chosen was quite a matter of indifference.

She then sang the romance; her success was the same, and when she had concluded, the young man whom she had before noticed again approached, and when Leontine found another piece of gold in her little basket, she justly attributed the gift to the generous amateur.

Madame de Rostain had left a letter with the Swiss porter of M. de Sannois, which contained her address, coupled with the name which she had assumed on her return to Paris; and had begged the man, if he could not immediately remit it, at least to send it to his master as soon as possible.

The Thursday following that of which we have last spoken, Leontine was thinking of a new visit to the boulevard, when early in the morning a carriage stopped before the passage in the Rue St. Denis. A gentleman of middle age descended from it, and inquired for Madame Dupré: that very evening Madame de Rostain found herself transported to a magnificent hotel in the Rue de Grenelle, where M. de Sannois lavished on her the most tender cares, and declared himself happy in furnishing an asylum to his beloved relations.

"I think I am dreaming, Leontine," said Madame de Rostain, whose strength seemed to revive amid this unexpected happiness.

" Ah, my dear mamma," replied Leontine, kissing the hands of her mother in transport, " judge if it was not the providence of God that came to our aid, for there was nothing left in the purse ! "

But the joy of the poor girl did not tempt her to add that the purse had been empty fifteen days before ; she feared the knowledge of what she had done would afflict her mother, and therefore kept her secret.

Meanwhile Mother Boudreau had received orders to bring to M. de Sannois' hotel on the following morning certain trifles belong-ing to Madame de Rostain, which were left behind on her hasty removal.

The good woman was exact to the time mentioned; and as she assisted Leontine to unpack and arrange the various articles in the drawers, she said, "I am very glad I have found you by yourself, Mademoiselle Dupré, for I have something to tell which will surprise you."

"What is it, then?" asked Leontine.

"Would you believe that yesterday evening, about eight o'clock, — yes, it must have been full eight o'clock, for the lamps had been lighted for some time, — as I was talking at our door with the man who sells chestnuts, there comes up to us a fine young man, dressed like a prince, to inquire about a young singer, who lodged, he said, in our house. He insisted upon it that he saw this singer turn down our passage last Thursday; and to convince him of his mistake, I was obliged to name all our lodgers to him, one after another."

"And did you mention my mother!" asked Leontine, greatly annoyed.

"Certainly," answered the old woman.

“Madame Dupré and her two daughters.
There was no harm in that, was there?”

“No,” returned Leontine, “if you were
discreet enough not to let him know our
present address.”

“Oh, I did not think,” said Mother Boudreau, with an air of embarrassment, “I did
not think there was any harm — ”

Madame de Rostain at that moment entered
the room, and Leontine made a signal to the
old woman to be silent, and was obliged to
let her go away without learning more, which
greatly distressed her.

There being no female to do the honors of
the house where M. de Sannois resided alone
with his son, he thought it proper for his
cousins to be attended in their own apartments till the health of Madame de Rostain
was sufficiently re-established to enable her
to come down to the dining-room with her
daughters.

The most tender and generous brother
could not have received a beloved sister into
his house with more delicacy and kindness

than was shown by M. de Sannois towards his unfortunate relation.

The very same day even he began to take the necessary steps to procure the erasure of Madame de Rostain's name from the list of the proscribed, and the restoration of a portion of her fortune.

" All looked well," he said, " for the success of the undertaking ; " and hope and joy being thus restored to the heart of the poor mother, her health began also to revive.

For the first two or three days, however, M. de Sannois did not speak of introducing his son ; but at length, finding Madame de Rostain much better, he asked her permission to present Gustavus de Sannois, who very much wished to become acquainted with his cousins.

" Though young and a soldier," he added, " Gustavus is prudent and discreet, and I have therefore thought it best to tell him everything, the more so that I chiefly reckon upon his assistance in obtaining what we want from the ministers."

After this explanation, M. de Sannois, the same evening, introduced his son in Madame de Rostain's apartment. To a very agreeable countenance Gustavus united a noble and elegant figure. It required but a very little time to ensure for him the good-will of Madame de Rostain and her daughters, towards whom he exhibited from the first more friendship than could have been expected from a relation till then unknown.

He regarded Madame de Rostain or Dupré with a look of extreme interest, and more than once he turned the conversation upon the obscure retreat where she had summoned up courage to live so long.

"It was my daughter who found courage for us all," said Madame de Rostain, pointing to Leontine. "But for her assistance, during the past year, I could not have lived."

Then, while Leontine looked down in confusion, Juliet repeated in full detail all that her good sister had done for their little household.

"Enough, enough, Juliet!" said Leon
tine; "all that was so simple that it is not
worth mentioning."

By degrees the scrutinizing looks of Gustavus were transferred from Madame de
Rostain to Leontine.

"Could it have been her who sung upon
the boulevard to support them?" he said to
himself with indescribable emotion.

He was very soon convinced of it, when
Madame de Rostain spoke of the period during which she had been unable to leave her
chamber.

After the first evening Gustavus went
every day to spend some hours with his
cousins. The more he became acquainted
with the virtue, intelligence, and good sense
of Leontine, the better he was able to comprehend, and very soon to partake in the
tender enthusiasm with which she inspired
her mother and sister.

He waited with a lively impatience for
the hour in which he might visit Madame de
Rostain's apartments, and to tell the truth,

Leontine, on her part, looked very often at the clock.

One evening the conversation turned upon music, and for the first time Gustavus ventured to ask Leontine whether she sung, a question which he had hitherto refrained from, without being able to explain to himself exactly why.

"Certainly she sings," replied Madame de Rostain, "and she sings well, too; for she had first-rate lessons in Italy. Leontine, my love," she added, "take your guitar and sing us something."

Since the last Thursday that poor Leontine had sung upon the boulevard, she had not touched her music, and the request of her mother confused her so much that she blushed deeply. Nevertheless, being apprehensive of exciting any suspicion, she endeavored to overcome her embarrassment, and rising with trembling limbs she fetched her guitar.

"What shall I sing?" she asked.

Gustavus then softly approached her.

"The romance of Nina," he said in a low voice.

The guitar fell from Leontine's hands as she exclaimed, "It was you, then,—oh, yes, it was you!"

It became necessary then to explain the whole story to Madame de Rostain, and the emotion she experienced may easily be imagined.

"God will bless you, my child!" she said, covering the brow of her daughter with kisses and tears.

The next morning M. de Sannois came to solicit the hand of Leontine for his son.

"What do you say, my friend?" answered Madame de Rostain, scarce able to conceal her joy. "Do you remember that you are a millionaire, and that I have nothing?"

"I have thought of everything," replied M. de Sannois, "and if our children have a family, Gustavus can leave them a hundred thousand livres of rent, and our dear Leontine can leave them her guitar."

THE MYSTERIOUS BENEFACTOR.

MADAME DE G——, a well-known Parisian lady, some years before the Revolution, undertook a journey to the foot of the Pyrenees, of which she has left an interesting account. The story, as we give it, is entirely authentic.

After crossing a part of the southern provinces of France, she reached the foot of that immense chain of mountains, so ridgy and picturesque, which separates that country from Spain. She took up her abode in a charming solitude, at a little distance from the valley of Campan, and hired a small cottage, where she proposed to pass the summer. Her little dwelling, situated on the declivity of a mountain covered with trees, plants, and herbage, was encircled with rocks and numerous springs. From thence it looked down upon a vast plain, intersected with canals formed by the torrents which precipitate themselves from the sides of the mountains. The neighborhood was inhabited only by husbandmen and shepherds. In this peaceful retreat Madame de G—— heard no other sounds but the majestic voice of nature, the rapid and imposing fall of cascades, the lowing of herds scattered over the meadows, the rustic tones of the flageolet, and the rural airs which the young shepherds sing while seated on the ridges of the mountains.

She spent the greater part of her time in walking through this beautiful country. She first traversed all the mountains within her reach. There she often met with flocks tended by children, or youths of perhaps fifteen years of age, and she remarked that the latter always occupied the highest parts of the mountains, while the younger children, who could not yet climb the steep and slippery rocks, guarded their flocks in pastures of more easy access. In proportion as she descended the mountains, she observed the shepherds decrease in stature and years; so much so, that on the little hills which bordered the plains she only met with little shepherds of eight or nine years old. Curious to know the reason of this gradation, Madame de G—— interrogated one of these children.

" Do you not sometimes drive your goats into the plains?" she said.

" I shall go some day, madame," he replied, smiling; " but a long time will elapse before that, for I must travel a long way."

" How?"

" I must first go to the top of the mountains, after that I shall work with my father, and then in sixty years I shall go down into the valley."

"What! are the shepherds in the meadows all old men?"

"Yes; our elder brothers are on the tops
of the mountains, and our grandfathers in
the plains."

Madame de G—— then left the child, and
descended into the beautiful and fertile valley of Campan, so well known to travellers.
It has often been celebrated, and well deserves to be so. We shall endeavor to give
an idea of it.

Let the reader figure to himself houses
scattered here and there, each surrounded
by its meadow, with a garden attached to it,
and shaded by clumps of trees. These
dwellings, spread over the valley, had gradually formed, as it were, accidentally, rich
and populous villages. The landscape is em-
bellished by the graceful windings of the
Adour, a river of a quick and impetuous
current, and whose waves, ruffled by a gentle
breeze, softly caress the verdant banks of
the stream. The cheerful frolics of the
herds, and the air of content imprinted on

the countenances of the shepherds, make the traveller long to take up his abode in this delicious spot. The valley consists of two lesser dales, one of which descends by Tourmale, and the other by mountains of the valley of Aure. Here we percieve the charming village of Bagnères, so famous for its mineral waters, and whither invalids resort twice in the year for the recovery of their health.

It was this beautiful country that Madame de G—— explored. In one of her walks she found herself near a cottage half consumed by fire, and of which the roofless and blackened walls presented a sad contrast with the smiling prospect around.

No living being appeared near. The trees which had hitherto lent their pleasant shade to the unfortunate inmates of this little domain, were entirely stripped of their foliage; the flames had not spared them, neither had it the grass of the meadow, which was also entirely burnt up. At this melancholy spectacle, Madame de G—— felt her heart oppressed, and sincerely commiserated the poor family which this disastrous event had driven from their parental home. She wished she could meet with one of them, in order to testify her compassion, and to leave them a trifling mark of the interest which she felt in their painful situation.

She had not walked many steps before she saw a young girl employing herself in spinning, whilst at the same time she tended a dozen goats which were browsing around her. The young shepherdess was seated at the foot of a mountain, cut down perpendicularly at that spot, and covered with moss and herbage. An enormous mass of rocks, placed directly above her at an elevation of a hundred feet, projected from the mountain, and formed a sort of rustic canopy. These rocks were covered with natural garlands of ivy, periwinkle, and bindweed, which fell on all sides in thick tufts and irregular festoons, beautifully grouped together with all the elegance and profusion of nature. At the distance of a few paces from the shepherdess were seen two weeping willows bending towards each other, mingling their pliant branches, and, casting their shade over a stream which glided down the mountain-side. The water, foaming as it flowed impetuously from its source, precipitated itself from the brow of the mountain over every obstacle that opposed its course; then babbling onward, it softly stole along a bed of fruitful herbage and flowers, and gliding by the foot of the youthful spinner, was at length lost in a gentle murmur at the bottom of the valley.

A melancholy sadness was imprinted on the features of the young shepherdess, and the sombre tranquility of her countenance betokened some recent sorrow. Madame de G—— advanced close to her, and asked her a few insignificant questions by way of commencing a conversation. The young girl rose up, and replied to her, using all the expressions of politeness which she could command, but still wearing the same dejected look as at first.

"My child," said Madame de G—— to

her, as she sat down beside her, " I have just seen a little way off the remains of a house which has been consumed by fire. If I am not mistaken, it is not long since this accident happened. It must have been a pretty place, judging from the picturesque appearance of the remains."

" Ah, madame!" said the young girl, while the tears ran rapidly down her cheeks; " yes, indeed, our house was very pretty, very convenient, very pleasant; but, alas! now — "

" How, my dear, did this cottage, then, belong to you? How sorry I am that I spoke of it!"

" It is no matter, my good lady, whether you spoke of it or not; that will not change our disaster. Judge whether I ought not to have been happy there. I was born in that house; my grandfather, my father and mother, my brother and sisters, and all our family lived there, united in the midst of peace and happiness. Now we are all dispersed — obliged to beg an asylum, which is not always granted to us. We have nothing left but a few acres of land and those goats you see browsing around me. Alas! what a terrible misfortune, above all, for my poor grandfather, who is so very old, and almost blind!"

"Did your grandfather, then, live with you?" said Madame de G——.

"Yes, madame; he has been a widower for three years, and feeling his strength decline from day to day, it was natural for him to retire from the labor of the fields. He had quitted the class of laborers, and had humbly resumed his shepherd's crook and scrip. In these meadows he had hoped to spend quietly the remainder of his days, but Heaven has ordained otherwise. Poor grandpapa!"

"Where is he, then, now?"

"He is at the house of one of our relations who is well off, but he cannot remain there long. Relationship is not always a reason for hospitality, and in a few days he will be obliged to seek another home. Alas!

it is painful for an aged man who has worked hard all his life to be forced to wander thus, without a stone to lay his head upon. But even, madame, if grandpapa should find a home, he will want something more to make him happy; he will not have his little granddaughter Lina to take care of him, to anticipate his wants, and to help him to tend his flock. Poor grandpapa, what an unhappy old age is reserved for him! He is so good and so virtuous!"

"My child, are not your father and mother as unfortunate as he?"

"Yes; and yet no. Yes, because it is as painful to them to see the work of their hands destroyed; and no, because they are yet young and robust, and can by time and patience regain what they have lost. But grandpapa is eighty years old. Happiness can never return to him."

"But by what unfortunate accident was your house burnt? Surely there is plenty of water here, and assistance could not have been wanting."

"Oh, my good lady! it was burnt by one more powerful than man. Lightning struck our little cottage, and in a few moments all our little property had disappeared, — house, crop, and cattle; and it was no less than a miracle that we escaped the same fate. It was by the will of God that it was done; but people say He only punishes the wicked; why then —"

"Yes, my child, it is true He punishes the wicked, but He sometimes tries the just, and on that account it is right to say to our heavenly Father, ' Thy will be done.' The triumph of a good man over adversity is that very resignation which becomes a Christian, and which, if properly borne, will conduce to his future reward."

"Oh, yes! I know this well by the example of my father and mother, my brothers and sisters. They are, however, well and strong, and able to work, and they will always find employment. I know also by myself, madame, for I was going very soon to marry a young man in this valley, who I

am sure would have made me happy. Now,
I have nothing left, and it cannot take place;
but I am resigned—all has no doubt happened for the best. I do not say that I am
not sorry; but I am sensible at the same
time that God will give me grace to support
this sacrifice. But with regard to my grandfather, he is so infirm and so near the brink
of the grave, how can he support the exile
to which he seems condemned?"

"Have confidence, my good girl; God is
good. We cannot penetrate into the secrets
of his providence. Perhaps the time is not
far distant when you will be recompensed
for all that you have suffered."

"My good lady, I accept the hopes which
you give me, and I thank you for your con-
solations."

"Have you not yourself, my child, some
means of assisting your grandfather? Could
you not occupy yourself, for instance, in
some kind of industry which would help to
procure him the succor which he requires?"

"Oh, if I only knew how to sing a little,

I should not be troubled about that! This is the season when so many fine ladies and gentlemen from the court and the town come to drink the waters. I would go every evening and take my place at the end of one of the promenades of Bagnères, and by singing for a couple of hours I should earn sufficient, and more than sufficient, for the support of my grandfather. But what is the use of talking about it? I cannot even sing a single song."

" Then you really think, my child, that by this means you could collect a little money? You are quite right, however; I did not think of it. But an idea now occurs to me, and I will put it into execution. Comfort yourself; I hope to be able soon to better your circumstances; only just tell me which is the best spot at Bagnères for a singer to attract a concourse of hearers."

" It is not difficult to find a good place; I can even see one from here. At a little distance from where they assemble to drink the waters, there is a terrace planted with willows, whither the company resort to enjoy the coolness of the evening. I would take up my station there, if only I were able to sing."

"Well, well," replied Madame de G——, quite affected, "I know of some one who can sing a little, and whom I will engage to sing for you at Bagnères. Here," she said, "in the meanwhile," as she placed some pieces of money in her hand, "is a trifle to meet your present wants."

The little shepherdess thanked her, shedding tears of gratitude.

"Will you be here every day, my child!"

"Yes, madame, I shall be here every day, from morning till night, spinning and guarding my sheep, unless one of our family be ill."

"Well, in a fortnight I shall come and see you to tell you the result of our attempt; until then do not be uneasy about your grandfather, for I think I can promise you that the future will recompense you for your present distress. Adieu, my child, adieu! I am happy to have met with you."

"Oh, it is I, ma'am, who ought to be happy!" said Lina, as she kissed her hands a thousand times, and watered them with her tears.

They parted, and Madame de G—— proceeded on her way home, repeating more than once to herself, "Happy patriarchal country! If felicity exists on earth, these are the manners and these the sentiments which will assure us of its existence. How happy shall I be, if my intentions on behalf of the interesting Lina and her family can be realized!"

CHAPTER II.

THE SINGER OF BAGNERES.

SOME days after this a report was circulated in Bagnères that a musician, who played on the harp to perfection and sung charmingly, came regularly every evening to give the most delightful serenades under the avenue of willow-trees. Nothing was spoken of at the waters but the wonderful musician, the exquisite taste she displayed in her execution, and the admirable expression which she gave to her songs. The applause was unanimous, and it was the opinion of every one that such unequalled talent would better grace the musical saloons of the metropolis than a public promenade at a watering-place. Those who had not yet heard the delightful strains of the new singer crowded to the promenade, and those who had heard her once wished to listen to her as often as they could, while the varied repertory of the skilful musician furnished a new attraction to Bagnères, and added infinitely to the number of the visitors.

As soon as evening arrived, the preludes of the mysterious songstress were heard, and then were suddenly to be seen groups of listeners hastening from all the different walks that led to the avenue of the willows, and grouping round the spot which she had chosen for her performance. The singer, plainly dressed, and with a veil thrown over her face to conceal her features, leaned with her back against a favorite tree. At a short distance in front was placed a capacious purse to tempt the generosity of listeners, upon which a little lantern, which stood beside it, threw its flickering light.

It may naturally be supposed that the mysterious circumstances accompanying the musician, — and especially the unusual talent which she displayed, — would excite the liveliest curiosity, and become subjects of general conjecture among the company. Sometimes people would follow her as she was returning home, in order to ascertain her place of residence and her name. But the strict incognito she preserved was proof against the closest scrutiny, and all their inquiries were in vain.

Sometimes it happened that the remarks of fashionable persons from the court were heard amidst the loud plaudits of the audience. "How fine is her style of singing! how perfect her execution! We can only compare this amateur to Madame de G——, and we could almost swear that she was that lady herself, if we were not sure that she was not at Bagnères. Her style, her taste, and her modulation are the same."

In the meantime, such was the delight with which these musical performances were received, and so captivated were the hearers of all ranks and of all tastes, that the money continued to flow abundantly into the open purse : the best evidence at once of the satisfaction and the generosity of the visitors.

This was, of course, the chief object the musician had in view. Generally her performances lasted an hour, after which the young harpist would lift the purse from the ground, take her instrument on her shoulder, her lantern in her hand, and without raising her veil make a graceful bow to the company, and retire amidst repeated applauses.

As soon as the fifteen days had elapsed, Madame de G—— hastened with the fortnight's receipts to the rock, which served for shelter to the artless Lina, and found her seated in the same spot as at the first interview.

"Here, here!" exclaimed she, "take courage, Lina. Heaven has not abandoned you. The person of whom I spoke to you has succeeded beyond my hopes. Here are eight hundred and fifty-five francs, the product of the fortnight's performance. You see, my child, that God never forsakes those who confide in him.”

“Oh, what a deal of money!” replied Lina, lost in surprise and gratitude. “Oh, how happy should I be to go and embrace the knees of that charitable person who has thus labored for our happiness!”

“We will think of that, by and by, my dear Lina; at present let us attend to what is most pressing. In the first place, you must give this money to your father, to enable him to repair your cottage. No time is to be lost while the weather is fine.”

“Oh, how pleased we shall all be!” replied Lina joyfully. “We shall be happy again, thanks to your goodness, and also to that of the person who, —”

“In another fortnight I shall see you again, and I hope that the receipts will not fall short of this day’s amount. One or two more fortnights such as this, and your misfortunes will be quite repaired.”

“Oh, yes, my good lady! Excuse me; I have not recovered from my surprise. It seems like a dream. I cannot believe so much happiness possible.”

“Calm yourself, my child; we must in this life know how to bear joy with as much moderation as grief. But, above all, seek your father, and let him neglect nothing to hasten on the work.”

“Oh, yes, ma’am; we shall all help, and very soon we shall have finished the repairs! You will see, ma’am, you will see at the end of the fortnight, when you return, how much we have done.”

As Lina finished these words, they heard in the distance the sounds of a rustic flageolet issuing from the summit of the mountain which overlooked the rock. Madame de G —— listened.

“Ah,” said Lina, smiling, “ it is Tobias, who is on the rock! he is playing my favorite air.”

Saying these words, she beat time to the measure, and gladness sparkled in her eyes.

“ It is my brother who tends the flocks of one of our neighbors, as he has none to watch over of our own.   I will go and tell him that soon, if it please God, his condition will be changed."

It was the hour of repast, — the hour at which the young peasant-girls were accustomed to bring the herdsmen their provisions. In the distance, on the other side of the valley, might be seen a troop of young girls slowly approaching, and dispersing themselves over the plains, while at the same moment the shepherds began to assemble on the heights, and to appear along the steep edges of the mountains. Some, leaning forward over the edge of the precipices, seemed every moment, to those below, as if they would cause the ground to slip from under their feet; others had climbed to the tops of the trees, to descry from afar the joyous band, which was expected every day at the · appointed hour. The flocks, left at this time to themselves, were allowed to wander as they pleased. Everything was in motion on the mountains and in the plains. The village girls separated from each other, and ran to seek their grandfathers, in order to carry to them the supply of fruit and cheese which they had brought in their pretty wicker-baskets; and the old men might be seen eagerly holding out their arms to receive them.   Madame de G—— stood still to enjoy this charming sight.

After staying several hours, and contemplating with emotion this animated and interesting scene, she took leave of Lina, not without again repeating to her what she had said about the repairs of the house.

We shall pass over in silence the transporting joy of the whole family when Lina delivered to her father the money which she had received, and related to him all the particulars of her happy meeting with the generous unknown.

They immediately set to work in good earnest with the repairs of the dilapidated house.   Workmen were put in requisition, and the traces of the damage had almost disappeared, under their united efforts, before the expiration of the fortnight agreed upon.

When Madame de G—— returned, and brought to Lina the amount of her earnings, which was more considerable than the first, she was agreeably surprised to see in place of blackened walls, discolored beams, and smoke-covered ruins, a pretty little cottage, with a smiling exterior, and a tastefully-arranged rural approach. There remained only now the roof to be finished; and the activity of the workmen showed that all would be completed in a few days.

Madame de G—— then made the acquaintance of this family, in whose welfare she had felt so deep an interest; and the grateful Lina was delighted to introduce to her, as their benefactress, all her relations — her father, mother, sisters, and brothers. These worthy people bore on their countenances the character of honesty and truth, and all expressed their obligations with the most touching marks of affection. Lina also conducted Madame de G—— to her grandfather. The old man was seated on a large arm-chair, which had just been purchased expressly for his use. His appearance was calm and dignified; his hair, of dazzling whiteness, fell in silvery locks on his broad shoulders; candor and goodness shone in his aged, features, and his serene countenance reflected the unalterable tranquillity of his soul. Lina, taking him affectionately by the hand, said, "Good papa, this is the benevolent lady who has come to see you."

"Ah, madame!" said the old man, rising with difficulty, "permit me to greet you as the saviour of our house. How grateful I feel for your kindness to my children! As for me, I shall carry a sweet remembrance of what you have done for us into the other world."

"My good old friend, I still hope to see you here a few years hence," replied Madame de G——, "when I intend, if nothing prevents, to revisit this delightful country."

"I trust you may, madame," replied the old man; "for I am truly happy in the midst of my children and grandchildren. But I am old, and God's will be done!"

Not wishing to detain these worthy people longer, Madame de G—— shortened her visit, which she would otherwise willingly have prolonged, so much pleasure did she derive from the contemplation of their patriarchal virtues. She then handed to Lina's father the amount of her last receipts, who was amazed at the sight of so many gold pieces, and exclaimed in his joy, " Really, madame, I think you are about to make me richer than I was before ! "

" Well," replied Madame de G——, " so much the better; you will be able the more easily to marry your good Lina, to whom I am happy to have been of some little use."

Saying these words, Madame de G—— left the house, and continued her walk on the mountains, in order to give herself up to the double charm of the contemplation of nature and meditation. Every evening she continued to take her place under the accustomed tree; every evening she excited the same admiration; every evening she never failed to receive considerable contributions. In spite of the lively curiosity which attached .itself to her person, nobody succeeded in penetrating her secret; no one, in fact, had known anything of her journey to the Pyrenees, and no one, therefore detected the well-known Madame de G—— in the mysterious singer of Bagnères. One evening, however, when she had just lifted her purse from the ground, and was on the point of taking her harp on her shoulders to retire, eight or ten village girls and boys suddenly breaking through the crowd, surrounded her, one exclaiming, " You have saved us from our misery ! " " We owe everything to you ! " cried another. " Madame, here is Lina, who wished to hear you," said a young girl in a tone of emotion. " Pardon her the liberty ; it was so natural."

Madame de G—— was not prepared for this outburst of gratitude, and she was for a moment disconcerted, as she perceived all the people approaching her to know what was the matter. Speedily recovering her presence of mind, however, she said, " You must make a mistake, my friends; I do not know what you want. You cannot know me, for I am quite a stranger in this country."

"But, nevertheless," replied Lina, "I assure you—"

"Undoubtedly some resemblance has given occasion to this mistake."

But Madame de G——finding these words insufficient to calm the tumult of emotion, bent down towards Lina, and whispered in her ear, "I beg of you, my child, return with your companions. This scene would be infinitely distressing to me, were it prolonged. I wish to remain quite unknown to these ladies and gentlemen. If you do what I ask you, you will oblige me, and in two or three days I will pay you a visit."

Lina understood perfectly what her benefactress desired, and hastened at once to fulfil her wishes. Then in a tone of feigned disappointment she said to her companions, "Let us go, my friends. There are many more singers in the town. I dare say we shall find another time the one we seek."

At the same time the whole party took the road to the valley, and left Madame de G—— at liberty to return to her retreat.

CHAPTER III.

THE NEW COTTAGE.

OME days after this incident the benevolent musician one fine morning
went to visit the parents of Lina. The cottage had now assumed a smiling aspect.
The building and repairs were quite finished,
and the garland of the masons, adorned with
ribbons, floated gaily from the top of the
highest chimney. Madame de G—— was
soon surrounded by the whole family; and
on remarking that all were dressed with unusual neatness, she thought that, perhaps,
they had some project in view which her
presence might disarrange. She accordingly
hastened to give Lina's father her fortnight's

receipts, which amounted to more even than the preceding ones.

" Madame," said the honest husbandman, " I shall accept this once the gift which you so kindly offer us, but I cannot accept it again ; it would be abusing your kindness ; for, thanks to your assistance, we are now richer than we were before the fire. Receive, then, our grateful thanks."

" Well, well, my friend, I shall not insist upon it. It happens, indeed, all the more conveniently, as I am obliged to go to Paris very soon. But do not let me disturb you, my good friends."

" Oh, but you do not disturb us ! " interrupted Lina ; we should be happy on the contrary, if you would pass the day with us ; your presence would complete our feast."

Madame de G—— having asked some questions about the proposed feast, now learned that Tobias, Lina's brother, was to quit the mountains, and that one of their uncles, who was seventy years old, was at the same time to leave the class of husband-

men, and enter into that of the shepherds.
At the time fixed for the ceremony, all the
people repaired to the plain. The old shepherds were assembled at the foot of the
mountain, where Tobias kept his flocks.
Soon after a troop of peasants and villagers,
drawn by curiosity, were seen running to
them. Madame de G—— mixed with the
crowd, leaning on the shoulders of Lina,
whose relations occupied the first rank in
this ceremony. The old uncle walked, surrounded by his sons. Arrived at the foot of
the mountain, the old man regarded in sadness the rugged path which led to the summit. He sighed, and after a moment's
silence said, " I ought, according to the
custom, to go myself to seek Tobias; but
my legs refuse to walk; I can but wait."

" Oh, father!" exclaimed his children,
" we can carry you; come!"

The crowd applauded, the old man smiled,
and his sons forming with their extended
arms a kind of sedan, raised him gently, and
commenced the march. When they arrived

at the end of their walk, they placed the old man on a rock. He rose up, supporting himself on his spade, which he had brought, and contemplated with pleasure the country which he looked down upon.

Tobias left his flocks, threw himself at the feet of his uncle, and the old man embraced him tenderly.

"Here, Tobias," said he, "take this spade, which has served me for more than fifty years. May you keep it as long as I have!"

Saying these words, he gave the spade to Tobias, and asked for his crook in exchange.

"Oh, uncle!" added the young man, "accept with my crook this faithful dog, which has obeyed me for seven years. For the future he will follow and watch over you; he can never serve me more usefully than by defending you."

They then descended into the valley, and Madame de G—— took leave of these good people, much pleased to have been able to contribute something to their happiness. In a few days she quitted the valley of Campan, and returned to Paris. Three years afterward she again travelled into the mountains of the Pyrenees, and she did not fail to visit her old protéges. Lina had been married two years. Her grandfather, whom she had always taken so much care of, was still alive, and the prosperity of their house was still increasing.

Before the principal door of their cottage had been planted a young and beautiful acacia, and at the foot was a square stone, on which were engraven the words,

"To THE UNKNOWN BENEFACTOR."

AN UNEXPECTED MEETING.

PON the summit of a green and olive-clad hill in Epirus, stands the village of Senitsa, wooded round on all sides by pine-trees, elms, and alders. Before the entrance to the village is a spring of cool and limpid water, which an aged plane-tree overspreads with its shade, like an ever-watchful guardian, protecting it from the sunbeams; and affording a resting-place for the dwellers in the village. Bleating flocks are scattered over the emerald pastures that stretch round the olive grove, and sparrows bustle with noisy flight from bough to bough. The place is a little Eden.

But beyond the immediate beauty of the spot, the situation is yet further enhanced by other features. The houses which cover the crest of the hill give it a smooth and glistening appearance, so that the village bears a fanciful resemblance to the sinuous outline of a snake, and all the houses, and even the roads, fascinate the beholder with an indescribable charm and interest. The eye embraces a wide expanse of country. Southwards are seen the verdant shores of Thesprotia, and its endless succession of delicious vales; southwards, too, is visible the Ionian Sea. To the north-west is the blue gulf of Andria; to the north, the Cha-onian land, and the contiguous vale of Thesprotia curved into many a tortuous bend by the silver-waved Thyamis, which winds along like a gigantic serpent, and then, over against this, the olive-bearing Corcyra, whose proud fortresses seem like swans upon the waters. Here, in this lovely scene, reigns an impressive calm, social harmony and domestic cheerfulness. The lover of Nature gives himself wholly up to contemplation, and the soul is soothed and lulled in a flood of ineffable delight.

Towards the end of July, 183 –, about one o'clock in the afternoon, a young man of middle stature, clad as a sportsman, carrying on his shoulder a double-barrelled gun of costly manufacture, and followed by a couple of dogs, was slowly mounting this hill. He scarcely made a step onwards without turning round to look about him in all directions, and seemed in an ecstasy of pleasure and admiration at the magic beauty of the panorama which unfolded itself to his gaze, while his dogs went sniffing about the bushes, or ran ahead in different directions, ever and anon returning to their master's feet, and then following a while quietly at his heels. The look of the young sportsman was grave and sad, but dignified, and his expansive forehead and restless glance seemed to indicate at once ability, enterprise, and caution.

When he was near the village the sportsman stopped before the first house to salute the young girl who was standing before the door, and ask for leave to rest, and for some food ; but he remained motionless in admiration of her beauty. This damsel of twenty summers, of tall and graceful figure, wearing an Epirote costume, with a narrow red ribbon negligently bound round her black hair, from beneath which appeared her neck, whiter than a lily, might well have served as model for the Amazon of Phidias.

" What eyes ! what a face ! " murmured the stranger. "Abominable tyrants !" And he raised his hat and bowed to the girl.

"Vous êtes le bienvenu, monsieur," replied she, in French, to his silent greeting.

" Pardon me, mademoiselle, for saying so, but I find myself in a situation which is to be inexplicable, The country, the very spot, the scenery, your own unexpected apparition, the language of my country, fill me with astonishment, and for a moment I fancy I must be in the land of the nymphs.”

“Sir,” she answered again, with a frank smile which parted two coral lips and displayed between them two rows of teeth brighter than pearls, “you are in a village of the unhappy Epirus called Scnitsa, and before a girl born in this same village, and unhappy, like all her countryfolk.”

“And how, mademoiselle, did you come to know French?” questioned the stranger.

“It is my mother’s native tongue, monsieur.”

“Your mother’s!” repeated the young man, amazed. “Your mother’s! Your mother, then, was a Frenchwoman?”

“Yes, she is from the town of Gourdon in Guienne.”

“And your father?”

“My father is an Epirote, a Hellene, born like myself in this very village.”

In his desire to know the reason of this strange union, the stranger broke in with another question.

"Tell me," he said, "mademoiselle, I entreat, how comes a Frenchwoman to be married to a Greek Epirote here? I am at a loss to understand it."

"That, monsieur, is not told in a minute. You have come from the valley where the sun is rather too hot to be pleasant. I see you are suffering from the heat and are much in need of rest. May I ask if you are alone? for generally the foreign sportsmen who come here are accompanied by a servant or an interpreter."

"True," replied the sportsman, "and I am attended by an interpreter and a servant. But the interpreter has been attacked as if by fever, and the servant has taken him off to some shops along the seashore and remained there to be with him and tend him until I return. But you do not tell me about your mother."

"Be so good, monsieur, as to come into our poor cottage, and rest a while. It will not be long before my father returns, and he will satisfy your curiosity.

He always comes home at noon to breakfast.'

The young sportsman followed the damsel into the cottage, where he was struck by the cleanliness and neatness of the dwelling and its furniture.

" Mother, dear," said the girl, as she approached a venerable old woman who was seated on a wooden stool, occupied in spinning, " I bring you one of your countrymen."

" Un français ! un français !" cried the old woman, in pure French, and in her excitement she threw her work into a corner, saying : " Are you a Frenchman, monsieur — a compatriot ?" and with eyes filled with tears, she threw her arms around the visitor, and kissed him on the forehead. " Oh, cher enfant, whereabouts are you in this neighborhood ?" said she to him. " Mon Dieu ! quel bonheur pour moi !" and, overcome with joy, she continued weeping.

" Madame, your beautiful daughter told me just now that you were born in Gourdon in Guienne."

"Yes, my dear child, there I was born, and bred, and married."

" But I am at a loss to conceive how you come to be here," said the stranger.

" Sad events brought both of us, my husband and myself, here to this beloved village, in 1815."

" That is to say?"

" The defeat of the great Napoleon."

At the sound of these words, a deep gloom overspread the features of the young sportsman, and beads of sweat broke out glistening on his brow.

" And how could Napoleon's destiny affect you?"

" How, my child? The emperor was our master. My husband served in the grand army in the regiment of Mamelukes. How? you ask," and with a deep sigh she again broke into tears.

The young sportsman, visibly moved, turned the conversation, leaving the history to be completed by the husband when he came home.

"Are you happy, madame, in this country?" he asked.

"Happy?" repeated the old woman, with emotion. "Yes, I am happy; the worthy people of this country are good to me beyond measure, and show me every respect. When they first learned that I was a Frenchwoman, there was nothing they were not ready to do to afford me pleasure. My excellent husband found a thousand ways of delighting me."

"The Epirotes are hospitable," said the stranger.

"Hospitable they are, my son, and honorable and courageous; but they live under a barbarous yoke. What can they do? Epirus has been the nursery of heroism. Do you see yon mountain?" said she to him, in accents of enthusiasm, and taking him by the hand she lead him outside the house. "Upon that mountain stands the celebrated Soulium, the land of the very Amazons. There, though conquered by the tyrant of Epirus, Ali Pasha came like another Hippolyta, the mother of the hero, Isabella, at the head of five hundred Souliote women, and slew or routed the troops of that miscreant. Further to the north is another warlike people, another people of heroes, the Chimariotes; and beyond this again, towards the north-east, do you see that long crest curved like a scythe? There lies Samarina, the land of a brave and warlike folk. And what part of Epirus does not emulate the others in valor?"

"And are they Hellenes?" asked the young man, pretending ignorance.

"Certainly," answered the old woman with enthusiasm, and with French vivacity. "Certainly they are Hellenes. They fought most heroically for the independence of Greece, a few years ago, and my beloved husband himself was at the head of a small band, and fought in various places. How could the Thessalians not do the same?"

"And what has Greece given your husband?"

"What could poor Greece give him? It gave him what she could, — a small payment. Sir, the whole Greek people were fighting for their country, and I am convinced that, were she able, Greece, once free, would fain reward all her children ; but, however much she might desire this, she would be unable to accomplish her wish, even if she were sold ten times over. Diplomacy has created this little kingdom, only to be crushed under the weight of many obligations and unavoidable debts, and be constantly the object of quarrels, demands, complaints, and jealousies."

" Tell me, if you please, madame, are the Thessalians Hellenes?"

" Heavens! is it possible that you Europeans do not know that the Epirotes, and the Thessalians, and the Macedonians, and the Thracians, and many peoples in Asia·Minor besides, are all Hellenes?"

" And how many Hellenes and how many Ottomans do you suppose there are in those provinces?"

" In Epirus and in Macedonia about two-thirds of the inhabitants are Hellenes, and about one-third Ottomans. In Thessaly, one-eight only are Ottomans. In Asia Minor, I am unable, my son, to tell you what is the proportion."

"I see, madame," said the young man, "that you are acquainted both with Greek geography and with the modern history of Greece."

"How, my dear child, should I be ignorant of the history of the nation among whom I have been so many years? With my husband a Greek, and my daughter a Greek, and having lived in the celebrated Missolonghi, and in many other parts of Greece since the war of independence."

"May I inquire, madame, the names of your husband and of your daughter?"

"My husband's name is George Kazoules, and my daughter's Hortensia."

The young man's breathing became more rapid, his eyes opened and closed spasmodically, as if in an endeavor to restrain a tear.

"I see, my child," said the old lady, "that you are overcome with fatigue and have need of rest; pardon me, and excuse my garrulity."

Hortensia, who had left the house a short while before, now returned, carrying a tray, and upon it a vessel of refreshing beverage, and a bowl of milk, and bread of the whitest.

"Take some refreshment, sir," she said to the stranger; "I beg you to let this serve until we can prepare an Epirote supper. My father will soon return."

"Hortensia, Hortensia, beautiful Hortensia! I like to repeat your name, I thank you, and he raised his eyes to the roof to dispel the agitation which he felt at his heart; then, quaffing at a draught the contents of the cup, he fell to with great appetite.

Shortly after this, a measured step was heard, and a man of sixty years, of lofty stature, and still as upright and bold in attitude as a statue, entered. His thick whitish moustache, which stood out like a brush from each cheek, his broad and open forehead, his fine martial face, a scar extending nearly across one cheek, proclaimed a veteran in the *grande armeé* of the Emperor.

The young sportsman as soon as he saw him felt there was before him an old soldier who had adopted the Hellenic costume, and was wandering about among the groves of the Kerameikos.

"Oh! Oh!" exclaimed two voices simultaneously, the voice of George, and the voice of the sportsman. Their salutation took place in silence — a pressure of the hands, embraces and sighs of pleasure, a greeting from soul to soul, a greeting of inward sympathy, earnest, sincere, for when hearts greet each other, the lips are mute.

"My dear father," said Hortensia, accosting her father, "our young guest is a Frenchman."

"I know; his men in the shops below told me so, and I therefore made haste and came quicker than usual. Eat, sir," said he, turning to the stranger, "and afterwards we shall have time to talk."

"I am going away shortly."

"I inquired of the men of your boat, sir, when you were going to leave, and they replied that it would be impossible to do so to-day, but that they would be able to do so to-morrow with the land breeze. Take some breakfast, then, and rest, and when you awake we can converse at length, for my wife told me that you wished to learn how I came to be here; and afterwards we will sup in Epirote fashion."

"Sir," said the guest graciously, "I obey you, and gladly accept your invitation to sup, but come and breakfast yourselves."

"Hortensia and I," answered the old lady, "breakfast at ten o'clock, so that we have finished long ago. Let George eat."

George sat down to table, but rather to attend to his visitor than to eat himself. After the meal the couple and their daughter withdrew to another room, leaving the young sportsman to repose in quiet.

It was three o'clock in the afternoon. Beneath the plane-tree by the spring, the water of which fell plashing from the craggy rocks, sat our couple and their guest, upon a stone bench which the rustic admirers of this beautiful landscape had set up many years previously, on purpose to afford a resting-place to those who went to the spring. The young Frenchman was smoking with thorough enjoyment a Havana cigar, while Hortensia was coming towards them at some distance, like a veritable wood-nymph, and bringing a tray with coffee, and coffee-things. She approached and poured out the coffee into her cup, and presented it to the guest and to her parents.

"It is time, sir, I think," said the visitor, "for you to tell me how you come to be here with my fellow-citizen."

"My dear sir," answered George, "I went while still a lad to Egypt, and there attached myself to the gardener of Soukiour Bey, one of the richest and most powerful Mamelukes in Cairo; and from this skilful head gardener, who was a Neapolitan, I learned the art of gardening, and when some years later he died, I succeeded to his place as the most expert of all the others. When the then General Bonaparte came to

Egypt, he wished to form a regiment of Mamelukes from the resident Greeks. In this regiment I served, while the army remained in Egypt, and when it returned to France, I went with it. Bonaparte was fond of this regiment, and when he was proclaimed Consul, and afterwards Emperor, he continued to care specially for it. The Mamelukes generally fought near him, for he was extremely attached to them on account of their courage and their devotion to him. At the battle of Leipzig I received this wound, of which you see the scar on my cheek, and for this distinction he conferred upon me the decoration of the Legion of Honor and promoted me to the rank of brigadier, owing, as I afterwards learned, to the mediation of a certain great lady. I fought in thirty-two battles, and I bear six wounds on different parts of my body. Upon the accession of the Bourbons to the French throne, I did not wish to continue to serve, so I took my wife, who I had married only a few months before, and came into this country where I was born."

"But you are leaving out the most interesting episode of your life," said the guest, smiling.

"I understand,—you mean my marriage. Joseph Loret was my intimate friend. He had lost his right hand in the engagement at Smolensk, and had been placed among the soldiers withdrawn from service by the Emperor, who had subsequently conferred upon him the decoration of the Legion of Honor, and given him a handsome pension for life. When the Emperor returned from the Island of Elba to France, he sent me with important despatches to the commune of Gourdon in Guienne, where I stayed twenty days, and then, having accomplished the object of my mission, I returned to Paris with the answer of the Governor. Of course I saw every day my friend Loret, who was then living in his native village of Gourdon. He had three children, one son and two daughters. Louisa, the eldest, who is my wife, was beautiful." The old woman's neck rose with coquetry as she laughed heartily; for the fair sex, even at the close of life, likes to hear the beauty of its youthful years praised.

"Yes," said George, casting a glance of sympathy and affection at his aged wife, "my Louisa was beautiful, and I was handsome and brave; we fell in love at sight. Love seized upon us directly, as a spark is instantaneously kindled from the flint. We knew each other at once. She wished to marry me, and I her, and that was the whole matter in a nutshell. I asked her father; he did not say no, for, knowing my military deserts, he believed that I should shortly receive promotion of some kind. My Louisa did not make any similar calculations as it was George, and not a captaincy that she loved. Love does not study logic; it has its own particular computations, which it demonstrates with great ease without one's breaking one's head over figures. Five days later I was betrothed, and afterwards returned to Paris, leaving my future wife with her father.

"Did the marriage come off, George?"

asked Louisa, with a native French gaiety, and casting upon her husband a glance which any man, who understood women, must envy him.

"Yes, my Louisa, you are my love of 1815," answered George, sucking the wine from his mustachios.

"Do not recall those times, we have grown old."

"Love is ever young," retorted George.

By four o'clock in the afternoon the table had been got ready by the beautiful Hortensia; it was covered with a snow-white cloth, and bespoke cleanliness and frugality. The knives and forks were polished as brightly as if they had but newly come from the maker. A lamb cooked whole, according to the Hellenic *cuisine*, in which the Epirotes excel, was in a pewter dish and occupied the centre of the table; the glasses shone with cleanness, and the wine of Zitse in its flagon looked like a colossal bulb of ruby. The guest was placed between the two aged spouses, and Hortensia sat opposite to him.

A girl from the neighborhood, who had come out of friendship for Hortensia to wait upon them, brought in a bowl of capon broth, made with giblets, wild aromatic herbs, a little rice, and yolks of eggs.

"What bright-colored soup!" said the young sportsman; "it is delicious, it is the first time I have eaten such soup."

"You are hungry, sir, that is the reason it seems so good," answered George.

"Not so, I assure you," rejoined the youth; "the soup is indeed excellent."

"Yes," put in the old woman, laughing, "it is the Emperor's soup, the same he used to call Florentine, and of which he was extremely fond. But your praises are in jest."

"Why so, madame? If Emperors prepared their own meals, their cookery might indeed deserve ridicule, but it is otherwise, for their cooking is done by common folk."

"I am glad, sir," said Hortensia, "that you give me reason to be proud of my housekeeping."

The young man inclined his head, and
confirmed the beautiful girl's phrase by a
grave and kindly smile. "My dear Angel-
icula, put one capon in a dish," said Hortensia, addressing the girl who was waiting on
them; "and do thou, father, cut off a shoulder and a leg of the lamb, to be set aside,
and put in the boat to-morrow morning.

"I am much obliged, mademoiselle, but I
think, indeed, you are troubling yourself
quite unnecessarily," said the guest.

"Sir," replied Hortensia with vivacity,
"we are masters in our own house, and
free to treat our guest as pleases us." And
as she smiled, she showed the sportsman a
pair of lips which seemed to part like the
petals of a rosebud before the beams of
the morning sun.

In this wise the meal passed. The stranger ate with huge appetite, and proclaimed
the praises of the roast lamb to such an
extent that, had the soup been endowed
with feeling, it would assuredly have pro-
tested.

"Life may be found pleasant every-where," remarked the stranger.

"Ah, sir, slavery and a pleasant life are two terrible enemies," answered Hortensia, and her bosom of alabaster heaved with a deep sigh.

"I'm going to drink to the health of a certain great lady," exclaimed George, radiant with the glow of the wine of Zitse. "Fill your glasses, you shall drain them to the bottom. We will drink to the health of an angel; and, raising his glass above his head, he cried, "To the health of the Empress Hortensia; may God guard her wherever she is!"

The young sportsman's hand shook like the hand of a man in a fever, and the greater part of the wine in his glass fell upon the the table, but, resuming his grave and calm demeanor, —

"Monsieur George," said he, "you appear to have a great devotion towards the Empress Hortensia, for you have given your beautiful daughter her name. I should like

to know the reason of such great devotion."

"I see you have made up your mind to
hear my whole life," answered George, laughing. "After the battle of Wagram, then,
when we had brought the Austrians to reason, we returned triumphant to Paris."

George recalled the days of his youth
with pleasure, and began to sing in French a
military song which had used to be continually on the lips of the soldiers of the grand
army.

"Continue your narration," said the young
stranger, with enthusiasm, to George.

"Well," resumed the later, "the Emperor
wished to change the Empress Josephine's
guard of honor at Malmaison, and despatched
thither a detachment, of which I, with one
brigade, formed part. I used to see every
day this good and virtuous lady, to whom
the army was passionately attached on account of her rare qualities. Not a day
passed without her showing us some kindness. If one of us happened to be ill, she

did us the honor to come and visit us in person, and console us, and took care that even the least trifle should not be wanting to our comfort. One day in autumn, as I was walking about the shrubberies at Malmaison, I came to a part planted with flowering shrubs, and, taking a knife from my pocket, I cut away some branches which required pruning. A shadow made me aware that some one was standing behind me, and turning round, I saw a beautiful young woman of dignified appearance, elegantly but simply dressed, whom I beheld for the first time; and I uncovered my head and bowed to her.

" ' Que faites-vous là, monsieur?' she asked me, in a sweet and melodious voice.

" ' I am pruning the shrubs, madame.'

" ' I see you are an expert at it; you seem to understand gardening.'

" ' I was a gardener before I was a soldier, madame.' When she heard this, she was desirous of hearing, what you have just asked to be told, the vicissitudes of my life.

" ' Are you a Frenchman?'" she asked.

"'Madame, I am now a Frenchman, for I am in the service of the Emperor of France. I am, however, a Greek, as I was born in Greece.'

"'You descend from a great nation. I have read his history. My mother made me read the Abbé Bartholommé's *Jeune Anacharsis*. What a people, what a nation, what sages, what soldiers!'

"'But now this nation is oppressed beneath a barbarous yoke.'

"'Nations which have such a glorious past and such a brilliant history as the Greeks are not doomed to extinction, as Providence will one day show . . . the Emperor . . . Oh, how I love Greece since I have read its wonderful history!' Her speech became broken, her voice sank lower and grew more agitated. She threw a purse full of gold coins at my feet, and with rapid steps disappeared before I could express my thanks to her."

" And then?" asked the youth with impatience.

"Have patience, dear sir;" answered George. "You seem wonderfully eager."

"And then?"

"You shall hear. And then, next day, lo and behold, a document comes to me: I am made a lieutenant with two silver epaulettes. A few days later, whilst in the garden with a comrade, I observe the same lady walking at some distance off. 'Tell me,' I said, 'pray, do you know who that lady is?'

"'What! do you not know who that is?' said he: 'that is Queen Hortensia, of Holland.'

"I resolved to throw myself at her feet, as a manifestation of my respect for her, and to express my gratitude towards her, for I felt convinced, beyond a doubt, that her Majesty had been the mediatrix of my promotion. She passed, however, into another part of the shrubbery, and disappeared among the mazes of the plantation."

There was something in this relation that moved the young sportsman, who was listening to it, so deeply that he was scarcely able to restrain his tears.

"My beloved France!" he cried, "my beloved people of France!" he cried. "Oh, how I love you!"

"You recollect, my dear child, our beloved country," said the aged Louisa. "You do rightly; and it is frequently present in my recollection. Would that the people of these parts could say the like, who have, and yet have not a fatherland."

"God, madame, who is the common father of ail, will have them in his keeping, and his providence is infinitely great."

"True, my child, it is great; but Europe — Christian Europe — forsakes us. Bless the prince who shall stretch out his right hand to this people! The great Alexander went to Asia to spread civilization there, and by that alone earned the appellation of Great. The name of the leader, however, who shall deliver the descendants of that hero, will be written more brightly on the pages of history than that of Alexander, for he will rouse the Hellenic people from slavery, and raise a beacon to show the East the light of civilization.   This man shall be called a benefactor to the human race.”

“ God will raise such a one up in His own good time,” answered the stranger slowly, and with a tone of conviction.

“ Give me the bone,” said George ; “ let me see your shoulder-blade fortune.”

“ So you understand foretelling by shoulder-blades, George ?   And do you believe in it ? ”

“ Just listen ; do I believe ?   Look at a shoulder-bone when you will, it will always tell you the truth.   The shoulder-blade bone is infallible ; ” and taking it into his hands, he wiped it.   “ I will interrogate it respecting you.   I will see what it has to say about your journey. I place you on the right hand.”

“ Oh ! ho ! ” cried he, as he observed the bone with astonishment.   “ What do I see ? An eagle hovers over you, a great multitude of people is at your feet. Curious ! My friend, you are a great monarch, or will be one.   You have, however, many vicissitudes before you.”

The young sportsman smiled with his habitual reserve and gravity; then, looking at George, said:

"I see, George, that you believe absurdities, like little children, or like old folk."

"It is as I tell you, my dear child," answered George, in a tone of entire conviction, pushing up the ends of his moustache.

Every one was up early next morning. The guest, clad in his sporting suit, was standing in the middle of the room, examining his piece and straightening his ramrod. George was stowing some portions of lamb, the capon, and some bread, into a basket, and bore on his shoulders, like a soldier's haversack, a flask full of wine.

"Hortensia," said the stranger, approaching the girl who was standing near, "give me your hand; I must bid you farewell. Take this diamond, let it be your dowry;" and he placed upon her finger a costly ring in which was set a very large diamond. Hortensia was for refusing the present, but the stranger said to her, "Mademoiselle, you must not reject this gift;" and his utterance was so grave and commanding that Hortensia remained speechless, her gratitude to him finding its only expression in the inclination of her head.

"Sir," said George, "it is time to depart. We pray God grant you a favorable voyage, and watch over you, that you travel back, without mishap, to your country; but while I have told you my history, with the utmost exactness, you must, at least, tell us your name, that we may ever remember you."

"Louis Napoleon Bonaparte," answered the youth.

Louisa ran forward as to embrace him, but the sportsman, with quick stride, hastened towards the road leading to the shop by the waterside, and disappeared.

BREAD AND CHEESE.

CHAPTER I.

AT TABLE.

IT was five o'clock in the evening, and the officers of the garrison were assembling in the quarters of General Bruni. The morning had been spent in a grand review and gun practise on the *Place d'Armes*, and the display was to be crowned in the evening by a most cheerful banquet. The General was an old soldier, somewhat rough in external appearance, but frank, and of a noble and a generous heart. He moved about among his officers like a father among his children. "Captain," to me, "your company files, marches and dresses so easily and so correctly, that the flash of their pieces has the effect of a fiery serpent."

"Lieutenant," to another, "tell your boys that I watched them as they charged; they are the very type of the brave soldier."

The dinner hour was meanwhile drawing on, and the general, approaching a group in the enclosure of a window, and throwing away the end of a cigar, drew out his watch, looked at it intently for some moments, and at length exclaimed,—

"Bertino is rather slow to-day!" He had hardly finished the sentence when the folding doors were thrown open and a valet, cap in hand, announced that the dinner was ready. The general gave the signal to proceed, and stepped up to a youthful officer of stout, well-set frame, and wearing a heavy pair of moustaches. "My boy," he whispered into his ear, "you shall sit on my right hand."

A quarter of an hour had elapsed, and active operations were fairly begun at all points of the table; then followed a brandishing of carving knives, a wielding of forks, a rending of fowls, a stripping of bones, a crackling of pastry, which promised a combat, *a outrance*, and war to the death, without quarter; only that instead of blood, there was an abundant flow of wine, and the general din resolved itself into words and laughter. But the General in searching his pocket for a toothpick, discovered that his watch was missing. He felt about in every direction, searched all his pockets, then turning to a youthful captain who sat on his left he said, "My repeater has disappeared."

"General, you may have left it hanging at your bedpost. A few days ago a similar"—

"Not at all; I tell you, I had it in my hand just now, and I am not dreaming. Do you not remember that I looked at it a few

moments ago, near the window in the drawing-room.”

“ Yes I do, too well.”

“ And you, lieutenant?.”

“ I remember it.”

“ I hardly know what to think of it — we
are all soldiers, officers — and yet the fact
speaks for itself; the watch was here,” laying
his hand upon his fob; “ten minutes have
hardly passed, and it has disappeared.”

By this time the guests were beginning to
look as if stupefied, and each one began to
offer suggestions, but without the slightest
approach toward unravelling the strange
mystery. The captain, who sat next to the
general on one side, rose, and said with a
smile half comical, half disdainful, “ I should
be sorry that any one could suspect me. I
am next to the general, but not to play so
shabby, unparliamentary a trick as this.”
And putting his hands into his pockets he
turned them out to the seams.

“ Nor I,” said another.

“ Nor I.”

"Nor I." And each one in turn followed the captain's example, laughing and shaking out his pockets. The general, who had risen from his chair, as if to watch the search more closely, followed the operation with his eyes, and with a half smile hidden under his moustaches, tried to smooth over the matter and to turn it into a jest, as if he regretted his haste in uttering words which seemed too sharp and offensive. Only one was left, the young officer whom the general had placed at his right; but when his turn came, he changed countenance, a deep flush ran over his face and brow, which seemed to burn. Seeing all eyes turned toward him, amid the deepest silence, he excused himself briefly, expressing his regret at being unable to give any information as to the missing watch. The general remained almost breathless, the spirits of the party were completely damped; the words were few and exchanged at long intervals; they seemed afraid to look each other in the face. There was no sign of the usual coffee, liquors and cigars. Every one, and especially the general, seemed anxious to get away from the place, to breathe freely, and to discuss the mysterious occurrence. As soon as they had dispersed, the whole conversation turned upon Liofredo, the unfortunate lieutenant. Meetings in knots of two or three, they spoke in a low tone, and asked each other what the strange affair could mean. " Who would have thought it?"

" As for me, I do not believe him capable of such an action."

" Eh! He may have debts; and debts sometimes suggest diabolical counsels."

" Bah!" interrupted a third, "even for a man in debt it would be a senseless proceeding, it is impossible."

CHAPTER II.

LIOFREDO.

LIOFREDO was a young man of about twenty-seven, of good family, handsome person, elegant carriage and winning manners. His forehead was large, his eyes clear and calm, and his complexion even at that age, fresh and ruddy as that of a child; and as an offset to all, he wore a heavy pair of dark moustaches, which drooped gracefully to a point on either side, and accurately marked the division between the cheeks and the chin; this was the only weak ambition that Liofredo knew. These external graces of person, were more than matched by his noble qualities of heart; he was brave, frank, true, disinterested, and far above any thought of meanness.

At the Military Academy, if he was known as an accomplished rider and swordsman, his reputation was equally high as a scholar, and master of military science. On his first appearance in the army, he attracted the attention of all. Not that he made himself remarkable by novelties or peculiarities of disposition and manner; on the contrary, he fell in easily with all, and was a most cheerful and desirable companion; yet he did not throw himself without reserve, into all kinds of company; he was seldom seen in the theatre, less frequently at late entertainments, but he never spent a day without giving some hours to study. This was no secret, and those of his companions who sometimes rallied him about it, far from attributing it to littleness of heart, or a niggardly fear of expense, paid him the secret homage of sincere admiration. Besides, Liofredo held the rank of instructor among the officers, and whenever any one of them happened to be unable to do duty, he was always ready to take his place, and to expose himself to the inconveniencies of wind and weather, to serve a brother officer. While drilling the companies, he sometimes stood by the corporal, and gave the words of attention and manual; and woe to the sergeant who used a recruit roughly in his presence.

He also practised the young sub-lieutenant in fencing. Those who called upon him, generally found him in his modest apartment, furnished and decorated by his own taste and hand; the walls were covered with scenes of war, redoubts, intrenched camps, military strongholds, fortifications, and all manner of permanent or movable works. It was a real military museum. Amid so many warlike scenes, there was one picture of peaceful inspiration, a Madonna' of considerable size, and of sweetest expression, a photographed Sassoferrato. As soon as one of the young officers entered his room, he rose at once, received him with a cordial grasp of the hand, and an honest, open, kindly expression of friendship; then taking down the foils, he examined the button, and placed the instrument in the hand of the learner. It sometimes happened that while he was engaged with his pupils, his friends examined the titles of the books, which constituted the library of his little study; Montecuccoli, Borgo, Charles of Austria, Jomini, and many other Italian and foreign strategists. In the midst of all this earthly strategy, as if unconscious of the nature of their neighbors, lay some works treating of the tactics of heaven,—a copy of the Love of God, by Saint Francis of Sales, and an imitation, with gilt edges, but evidently much used and almost worn out. As they read the titles of these works, the young officers exchanged significant glances, or pointed them out silently to one another, and then turned to the fencers.

One afternoon, as Liofredo was unusually animated in the exercise, and was perspiring profusely, though he had thrown off his coat

before setting to work, his adversary aimed
a thrust at his breast, and came very near
pushing his point into his ribs; he parried
the blow, and sent the point over his left
shoulder; but he had not been quick enough
and the extremity of the foil grazing the
shoulder, tore away a large shred of linen
from his shirt. A silver crucifix of good
size, which hung upon his breast, was un-
fastened by the shock, and thrown violently
against the wall. One of the young men
who was present, picked it up with an expression of some surprise. But Liofredo
was in an instant at his side, and taking the
crucifix in his hand, he brushed it with his
sleeve, and replaced it upon his breast, in
the presence of all, saying to the one who
had handed it to him: "It was given me by
my mother on the day of my First Communion; I never lay it aside either in feigned or
in real battle, and I hope to die with it
here." And without more ado he returned
to his work.

Those of his pupils who were wealthy

remunerated him for his lessons, and he accepted it without any false shame; but if one of the others spoke to him of money: "My friend," said he, "'I use my hands and my foil to open my pores, and by way of a little exercise. Say no more about money, or we are no longer friends." And it was said so frankly and honestly that no one ever doubted the truth of his reasons.

But there was one trait of Liofredo's character which appeared to a perfection not only uncommon, but even wonderful: it was his affection for his aged mother. When there was any possibility of her residing in the place where he happened to be stationed, he never failed to secure respectable lodgings for her in the most healthy quarter of the city. After dinner the officers met in the café to play and to read the Gazette Militaire. But Liofredo generally spent that time in walking out with his aged mother; it was a beautiful sight to see with what care he measured his steps to hers, how he leaned towards her, that his tall form might be no inconvenience, and gave her his arm with an affectionate attention, that looked like the very triumph of filial love. The venerable old lady, when she saw by her side the noble form of her son, with his bright epaulettes, in a position which did him so much honor, and admired by all, seemed to regain all her youthful freshness and vigor. The mother who met them could not forbear saying, with a pardonable envy, "Happy is the mother, who has such a support in her declining years!" But the best sight of all was to see him accompany his mother to Mass on holidays. He always came in full uniform, went himself to bring a chair for the venerable lady, and taking off his sword, out of respect for the holy place, hung it at the back of a chair or bench. At the close of the service, he waited until the crowd had dispersed, and returned as he had come. When his position made it unadvisable to have his mother near him, he left her in charge of an old family servant, upon whose care and affection for her he could safely rely. He never failed to write to his mother at least once a week, and when it was possible, to visit her in person, on which occasions the happiness of both was at its height.

Such was Liofredo, and such was he known to be both by his equals and his superiors: such, too, was he in the eyes of Agnes, — Agnes the good, the amiable, the beautiful daughter of the general. Between him and Agnes there had long been a secret understanding; and expressions of love, as pure and honorable as it was deep and ardent, had passed between them; and now they hoped that heaven would soon crown their prayers with success, when the unfortunate affair of the watch threatened to blight all their fond anticipation. But what was the origin of that sentiment which was now threatened with extinction in those two noble hearts?

CHAPTER III.

AGNES AND THE BROOCH.

AGNES, the only daughter, the sole delight of her fond parents, was closing the fourth lustre of her young life. It was but a few years since she had ended her studies in a convent of the Ladies of the Sacred Heart, and she had not been long moving in society, when she found herself the object of assidious attentions from more youths than one. Towards the close of the season of Carnival, there was a private ball at the general's; and Agnes, who never went to balls, could not well refuse her presence at this domestic reunion. A young man, of noble family, who had just led her to a seat, after the last dance, while pretending to be engaged in restoring a brooch which she had dropped, addressed her in an undertone: "You must certainly have perceived ere now, what my sentiments towards you have always been; give me some answer; for if your heart does not deem me too unworthy of its affection, the very day that gives me this assurance, will make the general, your father, acquainted with my intentions and my request in your regard."

Agnes cast down her eyes, and replied, while a deep blush mantled her face and brow, "Sir, I esteem no one more than yourself, and I feel honored by your proposal; but I am not altogether at liberty, and I hope that you may meet with one more worthy of your affection."

Agnes' mother seemed during the short passage, to be absorbed in the music and quadrilles; besides, as mistress of the house, she was obliged to see that the usual refreshments were attended to by the servants in attendance; but, like a watchful and provident mother, she never lost sight of her daughter, especially while in the company of the young men who sought her presence. She had seen the brooch fall, and though she could not hear the words, the action of the youth who restored it, with a longer delay than was at all necessary in brushing and re-adjusting the pin, did not escape her attention, nor the deep blush which remained upon the countenance of Agnes, even after the departure of the gentleman, who left her silent and seemingly unconscious of everything around her. The mother understood that something had happened, but she kept her counsel, and awaited a favorable opportunity to speak.

On the first Sunday in Lent, Agnes had gone to church very early; in the evening, her mother finding herself alone with her, "My dear Agnes," said she, "you have now reached the age at which most young girls think of marriage" (here the blood began to appear in the cheeks of the maiden) ; "what is to be your future lot, I cannot say ; but if you have ever given the affections of your heart to one who may be worthy of your hand, you should certainly not conceal it from me, since I am your mother and love you most tenderly. Tell me plainly what was that affair of the brooch, and the mysterious conversation with the young gentleman in the corner, near the book-case, on the night of the ball?"

Agnes, though somewhat confused, frankly replied, "You have a right to know all that concerns me, and I am not ashamed to make it all known to you. The gentleman said so and so, and I gave him a decisive answer."

"A decisive answer? What did you say."

"That my affections were already given to another."

"But that was acting a little too hastily. I am very, very far, my dear child, from wishing to give you any advice unworthy either of you or of myself. Yet I cannot let this pass without reminding you that this young man is of a good family, excellent character, rich, and gifted with every attractive quality; and, to tell the truth, we are better off in honor than in wealth. You might have answered with more discretion: that you would think of the matter, that you must speak to your mother, or a hundred other little things of the same kind."

"I should not have told the truth," said Agnes.

"And why?" asked her mother.

"Because, in truth, it is no longer a matter of deliberation."

"No longer a matter of deliberation?" exclaimed the mother. "That is no reason. I think I know the true reason; and if you will acknowledge the truth, you have already given your heart to another, far inferior, Liofredo,—"

The mention of that name brought a deep blush to the cheeks of the young girl and she interposed, though in a most respectful tone. "It would be hard to determine which is the better or the worse; and now, as I should not wish to have the remembrance of any insincerity upon my conscience, I confess, mother, that my heart is given to Liofredo; I hope that God may grant our wishes, and that you will be satisfied."

"And is Liofredo acquainted with your feelings towards him?"

"I believe that he has no doubt about them."

"How did he discover them?" continued Agnes' interlocutor.

"We have very often met on the walks; and in going to Mass we have happened to enter more than once at the same moment; then he lowered his eyes and I pretended to be looking in my book; but I am afraid that my looks betrayed much more than I would have wished to show. One day he came to make a report to father, and finding me alone in the hall, he asked me if he might speak to you,—"

"Which he has not yet done," interrupted the mother.

"He was waiting for his captain's commission."

"But do you know well," continued the careful parent, "who this Liofredo is? He has a pretty name, and a fine pair of moustaches; and besides these, no lineage, not a foot of land to his name; and simply because he is a brave youth, will you be content to eke out your existence on a slender salary?"

"That never entered my mind," replied Agnes; "and, besides, I have no desire of becoming a princess. His captain's salary, and whatever trifle it may please you to allow me, will be more than enough, if I am with Liofredo. Have you not seen how kindly he supports his aged mother upon his arm, as though he had a bouquet of flowers! I made inquiries about him, and I was told that he is as careful of her as if she were a pearl, and attends her like a servant. Then I could not help saying to myself, ' I may have less jewelry, less ornaments, fewer liveries, but I shall have a noble and affectionate heart that will care for me sincerely.' Then I have seen him at church, at the sermons, behind the pillars; and when he comes in he blesses himself with the sign of the cross from one epaulette to the other; the priest at the altar could not do it better. And on the feasts of the Madonna, I know that he always comes to Communion early in the morning in the Church of the Friars, here at the Monte. Where can we find a truer nobleman?" Here Agnes' lips began to quiver, her eyes were fast filling, and two great tears rolled down her cheeks, now crimsoned with the hue of virtuous bashfulness.

The general's wife was a lady of truly Christian principles, and of no less discretion. She was convinced that her daughter had chosen what was most desirable, a true heart and a sterling virtue; and, as she thought of the noble and gentle manners of the poor, but yet promising, accomplished young officer, she believed that after all, she could not hope for a more desirable son-in-law. She accordingly said,—

" Agnes, there is no need for tears; I

should be sorry to give you any cause of grief, and your father, I hope, will offer no opposition. I shall take the first opportunity of speaking to him about it; meanwhile be careful, and give no occasion for remarks."

That same evening the general was acquainted with the whole matter. He at first seemed little disposed to incline to his wife's view of the subject, for he was of the opinion that his daughter, though not very richly dowered, could yet very reasonably look somewhat higher. "She has a noble heart," said he, "a finished education, she is as good and modest as an angel, attractive, and the daughter of a general; she can certainly expect the most desirable offers." Yet there was something in Liofredo which fell in with the general's disposition; and he finally yielded to the mother's arguments and said good-naturedly, "Agnes will do like you, and Liofredo like me. He is certainly a young man of the greatest promise, and as for the captaincy, I know that his name is on

the list in the minister's portfolio.   He will
not have to wait long for the nomination,
and, in fact, I could give the matter a push,
if need be."

CHAPTER IV.

FOUR STORMS IN AN HOUR.

SUCH was the position of affairs on the day of the review, on the Plaza d'Armes. The general had placed Liofredo next to him at table, for the express purpose of sounding his disposition more thoroughly in the increased openness and freedom from restraint generally felt in the convival enjoyment of a banquet. In his heart he already considered him as his son-in-law; still he had warned Agnes to be careful, and not to discover her feelings too openly. She obeyed as well as she could; and yet, when the poor girl saw the issue of the affair, which had begun in the playful self-searching, and the display of pockets, and marked

Liofredo's changed color, amid the deep silence, which then reigned about the festal board, she was seized with so violent a palpitation of the heart, that she was very near fainting. But God gave her strength to keep her self-command, during the short time that still remained, to the end of the meal; and as soon as she had risen from the table, she hurried to her own room, and fastening it on the inside, she burst into a flood of bitter tears. Her frame was shaken with convulsive sobs, and her trembling limbs refused to support her; she sunk upon a lounge, where she lay for some time, bathed in tears, and overwhelmed by her first great sorrow.

Upon a little table near the lounge on which Agnes had fallen, stood a Madonna della Consolata* of porcelain, of a most devout attitude, and affectionate expression. It had been given to her as a reward of merit, by her religious instructors, and for

* The Blessed Virgin is known, under this title, in a shrine of great renown at Turin.

their sake, as well as on account of her own devotion, she held it in the highest esteem. In the opening spring she used to set before it bouquets of fresh-flowers, — the earliest violets, the first anemones, and the sweetest roses and jonquils. Morning and evening, her long and pious devotions were performed at the feet of her Madonna; and in the times of her little trials, it was her custom to seek comfort and strength at her little shrine, where she would then recite the whole Rosary on her knees. In this hour of real sorrow, she raised her eyes almost unconsciously to the figure of her Mother, and suddenly a ray of light seemed to dart into her soul; she instinctively threw herself upon her knees, and raising her clasped hands in supplication towards the sweet Virgin, so truly the Consoler of the afflicted; the anguish of her heart found vent in a tender petition. " Oh, my sweet Mother, if thou hast ever helped me before in my troubles, come to my assistance now. Liofredo is certainly innocent; and as I

have loved him with a pure and holy affection, now help us both." And with her fair
head bowed at the feet of the Madonna, she
prayed fervently, though it was more by
silence than by words.

It was nearly a quarter of an hour before
Agnes rose from her knees ; feeling her soul
refreshed and strengthened by her prayer,
she bathed her face and eyes with cold water
— arranged her hair and put into a wastebasket some little pieces of unfinished needlework, and went to the sitting-room, where
she usually spent some moments after dinner,
either in embroidering, with her mother, or
in reading parts of some newspaper to her
father.

On this day, however, the general, without speaking a word to any one, had withdrawn immediately after dinner to his study.
Taking a sheet of paper, he folded it and
wrote :

LIEUTENANT :— I shall expect you at my
office at eight o'clock this evening.

He signed the brief summons, rung a

little bell, and handed the note to the man who answered the call, but with a lowering brow, which plainly showed the attendant that a storm was impending, and would not be long delayed. He contented himself, however, with a simple "Yes, sir," gave the military salute, and proceeded to Liofredo's quarters.

As soon as the man had left the room, the general, stretching himself out in his chair, leaned his cheek upon his left hand, clenched the other tightly, struck his desk violently, as he said, in a low, decided tone:

"Either Liofredo shall clear himself of every suspicion of this villany, or I shall make him rue the day when he incurred it. What! if a gentleman, an officer, may plunder his general in his own house, and at his table, what are we to do to the robber on the highway? And Agnes is insanely enamored of this fine fellow; and her mother, now too, is caught in the net! Why I ever consented to such a match! I was too quick by half. But, now I shall, once for all, remove this worm which is tormenting her."

With this resolution he rose and proceeded to the boudoir. Agnes remarked the frown and the hands resolutely clasped behind his back, as he crossed the room, without a word, and her heart fell. She saw the dark cloud above her, and awaited the storm in silence. The general spoke, in a voice rendered deep and trembling by his efforts to restrain his feelings, he began, by blaming himself for yielding so readily to their wishes; then turning to his wife, he warned her to be more careful for the future, in matters of such a nature, and never again to speak to him of any match until she had long and maturely deliberated upon the matter herself: that these were not matters to be considered in a day, and that it was not prudent to follow every fancy that flits through the brain of young girls, that she should carefully examine the character and habits of persons, for, although one who, at first sight, looked like a golden goblet, might turn out to be a worthless scamp. Then addressing his daughter, he continued:

"Agnes, you are but a child, and have not yet learned that all is not gold that glitters. Now see what shame would have fallen upon us all, had this hare-brained fancy of yours been known by any but our-selves; we should be the common talk of the city. Thank Heaven, I think that your folly is cured now, and so it must be, if you wish to call me father any more."

To enforce this last sentiment, the general stamped his foot with some energy, when a noise, as if something falling and rolling along the floor, was heard.

"The watch!" cried Agnes and her mother, in the same breath; "the watch!"

It was, in fact, the watch, which had evidently slipped through an unperceived rent in the general's fob, and slid into the lining. The sudden and energetic movement of the general had dislodged it, and rolling down to the floor, solved the whole mystery.

An explanation so plain, so complete, and

unanswerable, had caused a complete change of scene. And now began a counter move- ment. The mother heaved a deep sigh of relief, and joined her hands. Agnes picked up the watch, held it a moment at her ear, and exclaimed:

"Papa, it is not hurt: ah, papa!" she added, with a sigh, as she placed it in his hand, "that you should have made me suffer so! I knew very well that Liofredo couldn't be guilty of anything so base. I asked the Madonna to take the matter in hand, and she has heard me."

The heart of the poor father was besieged at once by a thousand different emotions. The most powerful one was a feeling of shame and sorrow at the very thought of having so unjustly pained his innocent child. Pater- nal love was working in his heart; his lips began to quiver, and he might have found it impossible to control his feelings had he not turned away, and hastily quitted the apart- ment.

As he was leaving the room, he remembered the laconic note, which he had written to the unfortunate young officer, of the effect it might have upon him, who had been guilty of no other fault than that of being his neighbor at table, and at his invitation, too. He would have wished to recall the messenger, but it was too late.

"And then," he repeated, "that noble young man is dishonored in the estimation of the whole garrison. Why did I not think of the natural solution, — that my fob might be torn? And even so, why could he not do like the others! It was a mere joke; the rest had all done it. True, the fault is all mine; but yet, with that haughty manner of his, he has brought the difficulty upon himself. However, he will soon be here, and then we can manage matters better by a *téte-à-téte*, and this evening or to-morrow I can easily make the necessary reparation, as there are a hundred ways."

While these events were passing at the general's, Liofredo was still tossed by the storm which had been raised about him. On reaching his quarters he threw his cap upon the lounge, and with his arms tightly folded over his breast, stood erect for a moment, and then began slowly shaking his head backward and forward. Then he began pacing the room with quick and heavy step; he paused from time to time, and fixed his eyes upon the ceiling or the floor, but with the look of a man who sees nothing. He continued for a long while to walk the floor like a caged lion, and buried in gloomy thoughts; then stopping suddenly before the table, he took up his little Kempis, and opening it at a venture, he read the words: "Where is thy faith? Stand firm and persevere. Be long suffering and constant; the consolation will come in good time." Closing the book, he raised his eyes to Heaven, and said:

"Lord, by thy mercy, my heart is pure; my honor is in thy hands; whatever fortune awaits me, be it for good or evil, shall leave me unmoved by its attack;" and to strengthen the resolution, he then pressed his crucifix close to his heart.

At this moment, the general's orderly arrived with the brief summons. The young lieutenant read the note without betraying the least emotion, and said in a steady, firm voice: " Tell the general I shall come without fail."

CHAPTER V:

A GENERAL CLEARING UP.

T was striking eight just as Liofredo was ushered into the presence of the general, who was somewhat surprised at his composure, since he could not certainly know anything about the finding of the watch; and besides, the general felt a little embarrassed at his own position. He felt like a criminal at the bar; the words died away on his lips, and he hardly knew how to open the conversation. However, he overcame himself sufficiently to utter the first greetings with some degree of cordiality and affection.

Liofredo awaited the attack with calmness

and silence. But there was no attack. The general began by expressing his regret for the occurrence at the table, assured him of his personal esteem, excused himself for having allowed the game to go so far, declaring that he would certainly have checked it had he foreseen the consequences.

"Certainly," replied Liofredo, "I was taken a little by surprise; and the affair took a more serious turn than was promised in the beginning. I am grateful, however, for this expression of good feeling on your part, general."

"I never had a moment's doubt on the subject of your honor," the general replied.

"I believe you," interrupted Liofredo, "I am too sure of my honor. I think that there is a sufficient disparity between my actions and those of a cut-purse, to save all danger of confusion."

"I perceive that you have been somewhat disturbed; I sympathize with you, and acknowledge that I have, indeed, given you sufficient occasion for it. But now, lieutenant, I beg of you to compose yourself; the affair occurred so-and-so. See how a mere trifle has spoiled all the pleasure of the day."

Liofredo breathed freely once more. His features assumed a more cheerful expression, though without showing what a heavy weight was removed from his heart; he continued:

"General, it has always been my endeavor to keep myself clear of every stain. My honor I commit to God; he cannot fail me in my need. At any rate, not every misfortune is sent for evil; let us consign this one to oblivion, and you have it in your power to afford me some happier days yet, I trust," exclaimed Liofredo.

"God grant it. But if I may, with propriety, make the request, I should like you to satisfy my curiosity on one point, before leaving the room."

"What may it be, sir?" asked the lieutenant.

"I repeat that I have no desire to pry into your secrets, but if you are free to tell it, what could hinder you from doing like the rest of the company? It was a mere joke, and all would have been over in a second."

"There was, and, I may say, there is, a reason," answered Liofredo. "I would not tell it to everybody; but, on condition that it remained enclosed in your breast, I feel that, on this occasion, I may intrust it to you. It is this: You know that my good mother is old and sickly. When we lodge together I provide for her necessities pretty completely, and we are not very badly off; but when we are separated, as is the case this year, I cannot well pay the expenses for both lodgings. Poor, dear mother! At the death of my father, she resolved to save the honor of our name; she paid every debt, and remained with untarnished honor and her own dowry. She kept me at the Literary Academy, though, for those three years she was obliged to put herself on short allowance of food, and at last paid the last cent in her purse. And now, could I leave her to take care of herself? I have calculated the expenses, and it needs so much to bring her to the end of the month; while I, on the other hand, cannot do without so much. The deficiency would amount to fifteen francs a month. True, I have some money, but not sufficient to make both ends meet. I have accordingly settled upon a fixed plan; the person with whom I board makes a deduction for the days on which I do not dine at home, and on two days of the week, since you wish to know it, I live on bread and cheese."

The general opened his eyes very wide, in evident astonishment. "Yes," continued the young man, "on bread and cheese. I take a long walk, and sit down by some spring in the country, where I eat my slender meal with the greatest satisfaction; and return with even greater satisfaction to my quarters. I am young and strong; my poor mother could not do without those fifteen francs; I owe them to her by a hundred different ways; and, even though I felt no other obligation, there is still that of the fourth commandment of God. After the review,

I had purchased my provisions. Your invitation surprised me with my dinner in my pocket; and, with it, I found myself seated at your table. Would you have me turn out my pockets, to make such a display before the whole regiment? And, even independently of this motive, I felt such an unconquerable repugnance for the whole proceeding, that I do not think that I could have brought myself to take part in it for any consideration. The man who does not believe my word, insults me too grossly."

The general was deeply moved. Unable longer to restrain his feelings of admiration, he seized the hand of the youthful officer, pressed it tightly between his own, and looked him full in the face.

"Liofredo," he said, with a trembling voice, "you are the best of sons, as you are also the bravest officer in my command. Let me beg of you to be my best friend."

"That may be now, if you desire it; but later,—"

"Let me be the first in that, too. Later,

too, your heart shall have its dearest hopes fulfilled. That you may also be my best friend, I consider you, from this moment, my son-in-law. Agnes is yours!"

"General!" exclaimed Liofredo. And here the emotions which filled his heart made it impossible for him to utter another word.

"Wait a moment," continued the general; "before you leave the house, it is my desire that you should be betrothed." With these words, he left the room, and returned in about twenty minutes, to summon Liofredo to the parlor, where he found the general's wife and Agnes. The young girl had made her preparations so hurriedly, that she had hardly time to throw herself on her knees before her dear Madonna, with the thanksgiving:

"Oh! Holy Virgin, the favor is full; I thank thee!"

The betrothal was made without display. One circumstance, however, deserves attention. Liofredo, wishing to make some little present to his bride, and finding nothing else at hand, drew out a rosary of coral beads, strung on silver wire, and threw it gracefully about the neck of his betrothed. The mother then remarked, with a smile :

"A new style of present for the soldier's bride. But now, Liofredo, you have something for me, too."

"And what may it be?" asked Liofredo.

"The bread of the fourth commandment."

"Oh! as to that,—"

"Yes, yes!" exclaimed both ladies, "we wish to see and taste it!"

"By good luck," said the young officer, "I have had neither the time, nor the thought, to put it away. Here is the blessed bread that could have served me so curious a turn." And he drew from his pocket a goodly slice of bread, and one of cheese, to correspond.

Agnes's mother received the paper containing this modest meal, and began to cut it into pieces, indulging, all the while, in humorous and playful remarks. Then, taking a large piece in her hand, she left the room, returning, after a moment's absence, with a costly gold casket, set with diamonds.

" Look, Agnes," said she, " in this casket I have deposited the bread, so delicious to the taste, and to the heart of a mother; and do you take care to keep it until my hair is grey, like that of Liofredo's mother."

She closed the casket, and handed it to Agnes, who sprang up, and threw herself upon her mother's neck.

On the next day, nothing was talked of but the betrothal of Liofredo and Agnes. After Easter, they stood before the altar, to receive the Church's blessing upon their union, by the Holy Sacrament of the Church. Envied of men, blessed by the angels; Agnes in white, Liofredo with the epaulettes of a captain.

THE OPAL STUD.

CHAPTER I.

AT the outbreak of the war, there lived on the Northern frontier of France, an humble widow (who once saw better days) and her family, consisting of an only son, and two younger daughters. Her son Jean Jacques (commonly called Jacques), a strapping young fellow of twenty, in his ardor and chivalry, had gone at the roll of the drum to defend his country — bidding farewell to his home, and begging his mother's blessing, he started off to join his comrades.

A sad household he left; before many weeks had elapsed they found themselves so unprotected from the inroads of the enemy, that they determined to move further into the interior; accordingly they gathered together their scanty relics of former decency, and travelled as best they could to the retired little village of P——, which they determined to make their home, and now in the midst of strangers they had to find employment of some kind wherewith to support themselves.

Mère Adele, as the widow was called, and her younger daughter Annette, found ample to do at home, and Marie, a young girl of seventeen, after ceaseless efforts, succeede i in getting a remunerative occupation. My story opens on her return home, with her first well-earned wages, delighted to think God had blessed her efforts to support those she loved so dearly.

"Oh, my good mother," said Marie, "what makes you look so sad? See, I have been well paid, and have ample to support us for some time; don't be fretful over Jacques; he is brave, and will return to do us all credit. Come, to-morrow will be Xmas Eve; let us have one of your old legends, whilst we sit up to our cheerful fire, and thank the Holy Virgin for all the comforts we have obtained through her intercession. It is bitter cold out, and the wind is piercing. I saw so many miserable, half-clad people on the road, that we must thank God for all we have; however, we are not in a very poor neighborhood. I think there must be some of the nobility living near us, for that big house towards the East, is lighted up so grand every night, and — oh! listen, hark, what noise is that?" all three voices cried at once. "Some one in distress!—there, hear the voice again,—it must be murder,—what shall we do?"

After waiting a moment, and hearing the same pitiful cry for help again, the brave and noble Marie could no longer delay. Devoutly blessing herself, and throwing something around her, she called for the lantern, saying: "That's a woman's voice, and we must help her. Annette, you stay with mother, whilst I see what I can do!"

"Oh! oh! my darling child," cried her mother, "do not uselessly expose yourself, not only to the fearful blast, but,"—

The rest of the sentence was unheard by Marie, for to think with her was to act. She had scarcely closed the door when the voice of distress directed her footsteps, whither she hastened, without a moment's thought of self-danger. Guided by the glimmer of her lantern, she made her way over to a crumbled wall, where, in the midst of a pile of rubbish sat a forlorn-looking object, still faintly calling for help. Marie approached and asked:

"What ails you, my good woman?"

"Oh, mon Dieu!" cried the startled woman, "I thought I was dead; but you frightened the life into me. Who are you, and who sent you? Come, help me up— take my hand—very, very easy. Oh, oh, my leg—my foot—stop, what shall I do?

I can't stand!" Saying which down she came flat, at the same time scattering a lot of parcels of all sizes and shapes around her. "What shall I do? What will Mlle. Victorine say! My day all gone, and half my young mistress's things lost or broken, that hateful Pierre, the only man left at the chateau, and he too lazy to go, and here I am with some of my bones broken, and not able to budge—ah! never mind, Mr. Pierre, Louise will pay you off yet; I'll let you see you'll not lord it over me—before Père Jean marries us—it is not too late yet to change my mind—there's Henri, he would have gone for me. I believe after all, its very well to have two strings to your bow —worthless, good-for-nothing Pierre."

During this soliloquy, Marie very quietly stooped, and commenced replacing the various articles, as best she could, in a high basket.

"Ah!" said Louise, "my little girl; you are a perfect angel to come out such a night as this; I would have died but for you, and if you can help me to reach that big mansion, I will repay you."

Then they held a consultation as to the best plan of proceeding, and at last Louise concluded to take off her beautiful, new crimson skirt and put all her chattels in it, and for Marie to draw her home in the basket; but that wonderful feat was intended for more Herculean arms than Marie's, and after several vain efforts to move the ponderous weight, the lady's maid concluded she would try to walk; so off they started. At every step she bemoaned her sprained ankle; bestowed a holy blessing on Pierre, and hoped the coffee would be good and hot for her on her arrival; and lastly, wondered if she had all her mistress's goods, and certainly both she and the goods were in a beautiful plight, to enter the halls of the chateau; but all journeys have an end, and after hobbling, resting, jumping and leaning on poor Marie, the two women reached the gate, where, after giving the bell a good pull, Louise kissed the hand of Marie and declared her to be a perfect angel to whom she owed her life.

"Come back here to-morrow," she said, "and ask for Louise, and I will reward you suitably. I wish I had something worth giving you now; hold — wait till I try!" And after diving into several almost bottomless pockets, she found there was something in one. "Here is a mere trifle to-night, but not half you deserve."

Which proffered gift Marie accepting with thanks, turned to start homeward, and began, as if to encourage herself on her dark, lonely journey, humming Santa Maria, etc., on hearing which, Louise declared:

"That girl has no troubles; I wish my foot was as light as her heart!"

The gate having at that moment been opened by the only man at the chateau, Pierre, whom we will leave to assist his lady-love upstairs, whilst listening to many fervent blessings most devoutly showered on him.

CHAPTER II.

POOR Marie, shivering from cold, and knowing but little of the neighborhood, with lantern in hand, picked her steps to the best advantage, praying that her Holy Mother would direct her footsteps. After a considerable walk she found herself at home ; and, going in suddenly, interrupted her mother and Annette in their prayers for her safety.

" Oh, thank God you have come ! What kept you so long ? We feared you were lost. Oh, how cold you are ! " said Annette, as she stirred the fire, and warmed a cup of coffee for the almost famished girl.

" I fear, my dear child," exclaimed her mother, " you will suffer from your act of folly."

" Well, mother, I don't expect to; I am much warmer now; and I am going to have a grand recompense by going up to the chateau to-morrow. That reminds me I have something here; I was so cold I quite forgot it." And then, feeling in her pocket, she brought forth all Louise had given her, and which consisted of a few trifling coins and a tiny box, which, on being opened, displayed a small but beautiful opal stud, which, to their simple eyes, seemed wonderful. " Now, mother, do you think," said Marie, as she held the gift up to the light, "I will suffer for my folly? And this is only a trifle for the present; however, I will not disturb Louise till I think her bruises are healed; but to-morrow I will take this to town with me, and get something handsome. Oh, what a fine thing it is to be rich. Why, this will bring us a little fortune."

" But, child, are you certain it is yours?' asked her mother.

"Indeed I am, mother," replied Marie. " The person I helped is maid to some grand lady, and she seemed truly grateful for my timely assistance, and told me to be sure to come up to the house to-morrow; but this will do us awhile."

Next morning Marie started on her various errands, and, among others she did not lose sight of the pawn-brokers. On making inquiries, she was directed to Mr. Leon's, whose establishment she easily found, and went in, quite proud of her anticipated fortune. Mr. Leon, a personage of very great importance in his own opinion, stood very quietly chatting at a back window to a friend of still greater importance in his own opinion. The entrance of the young girl interrupted their conversation.

"Well, Mlle., what do you wish?" asked Mr. Leon.

"I have an article here I wish to sell you; and, as I do not know its real value, I was directed to this place, you being a most reliable pawn-broker."

Mr. Leon felt flattered, and still he was slightly piqued at the hint expressed about

his profession, and taking the article from
Marie, he looked and re-looked at it, and
turned it in every light; at last, with a very
gracious smile, said,—

"I beg pardon, Mlle.; but may I ask, is
this another family relic?"

"Oh, no!" said the simple-minded girl;
"it was given me by a grand lady's waiting-
maid, whom I saved from perishing last
night."

At which little piece of information, Mr.
Pierre, our friend in the rear, elevated his
ears so as not to lose a syllable, at the same
time taking a peep from under his hat.

"Ah, very well," said Mr. Leon, suppress-
ing a laugh at the innocent one before him;
"be seated a few moments, while I examine
this more carefully."

Saying which, he left the shop, and as he
passed his important friend, he beckoned
him to follow; and when they reached an
outer room, he opened his hand, and displayed to the wondering gaze of Mr. Pierre
the opal stud.

" Ha, ha! this is fine, I just came in good time. Now, Mr. Leon, you keep her, whilst I step outside and bring a gendarme, who will settle her in quick order." So off marched our friend Pierre, muttering on his way, " Now I'll make Louise remember her impudence; worthless jade that she is. The idea of giving away my mistress's jewels! I'll summons her; sore foot and all her bruises put together, will not save her from my vengeance." And in five minutes he returned with a gendarme, a man of immense muscular frame, and a face beaming with good-nature. Seeing Marie looking so modest and innocent, his heart failed him; but having had matters previously explained by the officious Pierre, he neither wished to offend the self-opinionated personage, nor his young mistress, who was very rich; besides, his duty had to be done, so going quietly up to poor Marie, he said as gently as possible,—

" Come, Mlle., I am obliged to take you under my charge for awhile; follow me!" said the officer.

" Who are you, and what do you want with me ; and where am I to go ? " cried the poor girl in one breath. " I am here on business, and am waiting for Mr. Leon to return. I have nothing to do with you."

" Yes, Mlle. ; and I arrest you on the charge of stealing ; the quieter you follow me, the better for yourself ; if needed, I can force you."

" Oh, my God, what will I do ? " interrogated Marie ; " my poor mother and Annette, what will become of them ; it will kill them ! " and throwing herself on her knees, she begged the man to have pity on her, declaring she had stolen nothing.

" All this talk, Mlle., will do no good ; you can ask all these questions of the Magistrate, but I must do my duty."

Saying which, he placed his hand on her shoulder and forced her away, while she asked, at least to wait till she could get her money, showing evidently that the simple girl did not have the slightest suspicion why she was under arrest.

CHAPTER III.

THAT Christmas Eve, on which so much comfort was anticipated in Mère Adele's household, where were all its members? The poor widow and Annette, after spending a miserable day of torture and suspense, and inquiring in all directions for poor Marie, were compelled to return to their humble and desolate home, with their hearts nearly broken, there to watch till the break of day for the lost one. Oh, could they have peered through the rough wall of· Marie's prison cell; in the depth of their trouble, they would have known from her angelic appearance, that even in that dismal spot her heavenly angel was guarding her. There she knelt the greater part of the night, saying,—

"Oh, sweet Infant Jesus, before whom the shepherds bow in adoration to-night, have pity on me; deliver me from this cell, and have pity on my poor mother. Oh, gentle Mother of Jesus, thou who hast never forsaken me, beg thy Divine Infant to smile on me, and cheer my almost withered heart. Well might I cheerfully spend one night in a dungeon when He, the King of all, came for us into this miserable, cold world; making his advent in a bleak, comfortless stable."

Thus prayed Marie until from pure exhaustion she fell into a profound sleep, from which she did not awaken until she was aroused by a very loud knock, and immediately the gendarme walked in.

"Your slumbers must have been very heavy, Mlle.; thinking you were friendless, I got permission to see you, and having rapped repeatedly and receiving no answer, I was on the point of retiring, when I thought I would give a regular rouser, and come in to see what was the matter. You remind me of my own little sister at home, for I am a stranger here, and now what can I do for you? Have you no friend I can send you? Tell me quickly for my time is passing."

Marie's heart beat with joy as she surely thought the Infant Jesus had really smiled on her, and the Blessed Virgin procured her a friend.

"A thousand thanks!" exclaimed poor Marie; "you can do much for me. First, tell me why I am here."

"Why, you simple child," replied the gendarme, "do you not know that you are in prison on suspicion of stealing; having tried to sell Mr. Leon a valuable piece of jewelry belonging to Capt. L——. You will be tried to-morrow or after, and probably would like to have some advice."

"Oh, may God and the Blessed Virgin protect me from harm : it is the stud; now I will tell you all;" and Marie, in her quiet way, told her simple tale. Being innocent of locations, and knowing no name but that of Louise, her story was rather indefinite ; however, he believed her truthfulness, and one stranger having a kindred feeling for another, he determined to help her.

"Well," said he, "I will do what I can for you. Have you no relations?"

At which question the tears ran down Marie's cheeks, as she told of her mother and sister, naming where they lived.

"Well, don't fret, that will spoil your pretty face. I will do my best, and will see you again to-morrow."

I will now conduct my young reader to the chateau. There, in the well-lighted drawing-room, before a most inviting fire, sat Mlle. Victorine and her father, Capt. L——, who having been severely wounded, had returned home still an invalid, accompanied by his faithful servant, Jean. Whilst father and daughter enjoyed each other's society, the servants in the lower hall had grand rejoicings over their good master's return.

The captain's old body servant had been killed in a skirmish, and from his regiment his present attendant had been selected, who having twice saved his master's life, was naturally held in high esteem; so, although Jean was the only stranger that was around the blazing hearth; still he was the centre of all attention, as he rehearsed the wonderful feats he had witnessed. Then, to one side, the cook and her assistants, attending the savory pots for the approaching supper, and in the far corner sat our friend Pierre and convalescent Louise, who having forgiven each other's little failings, and settled their anti-matrimonial disputes, looked as loving as two cooing doves.

The attention of Jean's excited listeners was disturbed by a terrible ringing of the outer bell, such a pull as would say, "Don't keep me waiting." Even Pierre, loath as he was to leave his comfortable quarters, jumped up at once, and answered the call. On opening the gate he saw before him Marie's friend, the gendarme.

"Well, Mr. Pierre, I am delighted at last to have found you. I've been hunting the place for nearly an hour, and my legs are nearly frozen ! "

" Well," answered Pierre, " if we remain here, our noses will soon be the same ; come where we can get a snuff of the fire." So Pierre led the way through the long corridors, muttering as he went, " What impudence this fellow has to hunt me up." However, both their tempers improved as they inhaled the warm atmosphere of the kitchen, Pierre forgiving his having been disturbed, and his friend forgetting his nearly frozen legs. Now, sir," said consequential Pierre, " when you are warm I would like to know how I can serve you?"

To which the gendarme replied : " You can serve me well ; and the sooner we talk business the better. I want to know if you can help in any way, this poor young girl that you were the cause of my arresting. Her sweet, innocent face has haunted me ever since I laid my hand on her ; besides, I saw her mother and sister this evening, and to my perfect astonishment, I find her father and I were old friends. I would take my oath that no child of Louis Dubois would ever be guilty of theft; and as I believe her innocent, I will befriend her."

Louise, at this moment stood up and declared the girl to be entirely innocent, and explained how her own misfortunes had been the cause of all the trouble, and how satisfied her mistress was with the explanation she had given of the stud having, in the upset she got, fallen in her pocket; and she, in the dark having given it to Marie.

"Besides, the girl saved me from perishing, and I feel bound to do what I can for her. So Pierre and I will go to see her to-morrow, — what's her name?"

The gendarme standing up to go, replied, —

"Her name is Marie Dubois, and her mother and sister, Annette, live just beyond here. The old woman told me her son was fighting, and I will protect the friendless."

At the mention of all these names, Jean, (who was none other than Jean Jacques), stood like one petrified ; and, at last, making over to the gendarme, and shaking his hand heartily, said ;—

"If you are their friend, you must be mine ; for it must be of my mother and sister of whom you speak, although I left them far from here. Still the horrors of war may have deprived them of their home. I will go with you at once to decide the question ;" and starting without delay, they soon reached the widow Adele's cottage.

CHAPTER IV.

SCARCELY had the gate closed when the bell summoned Pierre to the drawing-room. The captain on seeing him, desired Jean to be sent to him, "For I have become so accustomed to his ways, that no one else can wait on me."

"Sir," replied Pierre, "he has gone to see his mother and sister who live below here."

"Why, if Jean turns liar, I am much mistaken in him," said the captain: "he told me his family lived on the frontier."

"Well, captain, I must explain it," said Pierre, and then again came out Marie's story, and Mlle. Victorine added, —

"This is the girl who was arrested for trying to sell the stud."

"Well, Pierre, I will await Jean's return; send him to me as soon as he comes; if it is his sister, I must befriend her."

An hour after Jacques returned truly happy at the most unexpected pleasure of having seen his mother and sister; but sad at heart on account of Marie.

Pierre having told his master's wishes, Jacques immediately presented himself before the captain, who having heard his recital, immediately called for both Louise and Pierre to hear their version, at the end of which tedious explanation, the captain addressing them, said,—

"As well as I understand the case, Pierre, you have acted too hastily, and without judgment; I may even add justice. You should have made inquiries before taking such a decided step; I fear a lecture from your lady-love has been the cause of your acting precipitately and also without the slightest consideration for others. However, I being a magistrate, and the parties being within my district, I may be able to undo the mischief of which you have mainly been the cause. To-morrow morning I will write an order for the release of Marie, and you, Pierre, accompanied by Louise, and my faithful servant, shall take the family coach and bring Marie, as well as the gendarme here, and in the presence of all I will examine the affair."

Early next morning Marie was perfectly surprised, by the fact being announced to her she was released; and still more astonished when, on being accompanied by the gendarme to the coach that awaited her, to find her brother seated therein. Her joy was almost overpowering; she would have believed it a dream, but for the embraces of her brother, and the cheering voice of Louise, whom she at once recognized. Her lips were motionless; all she could do was to give thanks from her heart, that the aid she had craved from the Infant Jesus had scattered all her past troubles. When they reached the chateau and Marie was informed she would have to appear before Capt.

L——, to whom the stud belonged, her fears
would have terrified her, but for the assurance, that justice should be done her. At
noon the captain commanded that his entire
household should appear in his presence.
After hearing the details of Louise's perilous
and unfortunate journey, also Marie's pre-
serving her from the terrors of the night, then
the selling of the stud and Pierre's interfer-
ence, he at once took the whole affair in at a
glance, and looking at Marie's pale, beautiful
countenance, he called her over to him, and
said, —

"My dear child, you have suffered much,
and as my property has been unwittingly
the cause of all your troubles, I feel bound
as far as I am able to repay you in some
measure for the pain of mind as well as of
body you have endured. You are now freed
from prison, and perfectly exonerated from
any dishonorable dealing. You may now
return to your mother; but before leaving,
I wish to know how I can serve you, what
do you most wish for?"

" Many thanks, my dear, good gentle-man, " said Marie, tears of gratitude stream-ing from her eyes as she spoke, " I wish for nothing but to return to. my home, truly thankful for all your kindness to me. Now, that my brother is at home I will, if pos-sible fly from the world altogether, and try to gain admittance into the Convent of Our Lady, to whose intercession I attribute my release, and the best I can do is, for the remainder of my life to bless her for her protection."

" Well, my dear girl," said the captain, " may I ask, how much money have you to admit you in the convent."

" None, captain," she replied, " I have no ambition above that of a lay sister. I can offer naught but the strength of my hands, and the poverty and willingness of my grate-ful heart."

" Such shall no longer be the case," re-plied the captain. " I am delighted to have it in my power to endow you with a fortune quite sufficient to have you placed amongst the choir-sisters, and will hand a check to your brother for that purpose. I will care for your mother and sister, who shall for the future belong to my tenantry. As for your brother I must keep him to attend my personal wants;" and here calling Jean, he said, "my faithful man, I can do no better with this stud than present it to you as a memento of the circumstances which have brought your worthy family fully to my knowledge. As for the noble-minded gendarme, he may rest assured his promotion shall be attended to without delay, and you Pierre and Louise, I think the best thing you can do is, as soon as possible, to give us the pleasure of attending your nuptials, thus putting an end to your spats, the effects of which you see can prove very dangerous. So now, my good people, before you disperse, Pierre will dispense the hospitalities of the house to you all below, and the first bumper you fill, let it be drunk to the health of Pierre and his bride elect."

Two months later, when the woods began

to resound with the early notes of myriads of birds, and snow-bound streams broke forth from their icy fetters, kissing, as they passed, the snowdrop and sweet violet on their mossy banks — in fact, one of those pet days when nature blooms forth in all her new-born beauty, Pierre led to the altar his blushing bride, Louise, for whom little Annette acted as bridesmaid, and Pierre's best man was no other than Jean Jacques, who on so important an occasion did not neglect to deck himself with the opal stud.

The ceremony was performed by Père Jean, who, knowing all the secrets of the bridal party was most careful to doubly knot the cord of wedlock, so that Madame Pierre in future would be fully assured, that there was no longer "two strings to her bow." The festive scene was graced by many guests, but none were more joyful than the good-hearted gendarme, who with his partner, Mère Adele, tripped lightly through the merry dance. And where was poor Marie? In her quiet cell she prayed that God would bless the happy pair, who, were the innocent cause of all her bitter trials; true those very trials had been the medium of bringing comfort to her family, and had proved to her the germ of the sweetest consolation which she enjoyed in obtaining the protection of the blessed Mother of God, and the priceless love of the sweet Infant Jesus.

ISABELLA.

"APRIL showers bring forth May flowers." Sometimes, when the seed has been sown in good soil, not too deep, or too near the surface, or too early. And as perpetual showers and unseasonable thunder storms will exercise an evil and destructive influence on the life and future growth of the embryo blossoms, so will the ever-recurring showers and thunder storms of an angry temper check the fairest promise, in that sweetest and most beautiful of all blossoms,—the heart of a young child.

It was a blessing for Isabella Hughes when her mother died: the expression may seem strange and unnatural, but it is none the less true. Her father, an intelligent young Englishman, of good family and excellent education, had left his native country, and incurred the displeasure of his only brother, a very wealthy man, in consequence of having embraced the Catholic faith, and having found a situation as teacher of mathematics at a private academy in Baltimore, also found board and lodging in the house of Mrs. Caroline Pettigrew, a widow without children, and who joined to a natural acidity of disposition, a most disagreeable propensity to fault-finding, and an iron will, which carried everything before its arbitrary sweep. Mr. Hughes had not been many weeks in her house when he was seized with typhoid fever, through the various stages of which he was assiduously nursed by his landlady, whose regard for him grew in proportion to his helplessness. Once convalescent, weak, spiritless, and grateful for her kindness, in debt, moreover, for board and medicine, he saw but one way in which to refund what he owed her : in short, he proposed marriage to Mrs. Pettigrew, and was accepted. After a few years, the poor man died, as he had not lived, in peace. Baby arms were around his neck in the last struggle, and " be good to her " were his last intelligible words.

Poor little Isabella, — her lot was henceforward to be cast in thorny ways. She did not resemble her mother in anything save he complexion and hair, which were fair. She had her father's eyes, blue and sparkling, his mobile lips and slender figure, and, alas, his sensitive disposition. From her earliest babyhood, her mother's quick, sharp tones would startle her ; and as Mrs. Hughes had a profound contempt for meekness in any shape or form, it is not wonderful she evinced no sympathy for Isabella's predominant trait.

" Isabella, child, come here this instant. Isabella, what are you dawdling about, up in that room. Isabella, get ready this very moment, and go to school. Isabella, is it your deliberate intention to be late for Mass?"

These were specimens of her kindest mode of address. But in her angry words, — and they were not unfrequent, — she was terrible.

Stamping her foot at the quiet, inoffensive child, she would shower forth invectives of all kinds, not always unaccompanied by blows; indeed, she appeared to make the little girl a target, at which to fire all the loose ammunition of her bad temper. Such a course was not without pernicious effects. From a shy, loving, and sensitive child, Isabella became silent, morbid, and sullen; harshness and unkindness were habitual to her, and, although she did not feel them less, her heart resented them more and more, as years passed on. She had few companions of her own age, her mother not approving of the association of the school children; "they were too frisky and foolish," she said. Isabella was clever, and inherited her father's talent for mathematics; but her reserved manner was not calculated to attract either teachers or companions. "A sullen, disagreeable girl," would be the verdict of a casual observer, who, overlooking the flexible lips and large, intelligent eyes, would only note the downcast face and cold, repellant expression.

Thus passed her loveless, early childhood, unconscious of any fairer, lighter existence outside her own. Isabella often wondered in what life was beautiful, and the sight of happy children always made her feel mean and annoyed. She was passionately fond of music, and on an old piano of her father's she had learned many an air, quite unassisted. Her mother would not permit her to take lessons, saying her means were too limited to allow of such extravagance, and on occasions, often forbade her to touch the instrument, for weeks together. Mrs. Hughes' unsocial disposition had always kept acquaintances at a distance, and Isabella's life was monotonous, indeed, until one fair, spring morning, an imperious visitor knocked at the door, and the hard, stern woman grew fearful and powerless before that hardest, sternest, most unwelcome guest named Death. A few hours of suffering, a hurried visit from priest and doctor, and Isabella Hughes stood at her mother's bedside an orphan and alone. She did not shed many tears at first, but after the shock had become in some degree familiar, all her pent-up feelings burst forth, and she wept, not so much at the loss of a mother, who had stifled all tender sentiments in her heart, as at the dreary prospect — the lack of love that lay before her.

After the funeral, the priest who had administered the last Sacraments to Mrs. Hughes, informed Isabella that he had her mother's will in his possession, saying, at the same time, that he hoped she was pleased with the arrangements for her future.

"I have not heard of any, father," said Isabella gravely, and without lifting her eyes.

"Is it possible, my child?" he answered, "are you not aware that your uncle in England left you a legacy some years ago, on condition that you should be placed at a convent school, from the age of fifteen to eighteen?"

"I did not know that I ever had an uncle in England, until now, father," said Isabella, her cheeks flushing slightly as she spoke.

"You knew your father was an Englishman, did you not, Isabella?"

"Yes, father; I heard my mother speaking of him once to Father Boyce; she said he had offended his family by becoming a Catholic. That is all I know of him."

"Did your mother never speak of him to you?"

"No, sir; my mother never spoke to me of anything. She did not believe in talking to children, she said."

"And do you remember your father? You were four years old when he died."

"I think I do, sir. Did he have blue eyes, and was he tall, and did he have very white hands?"

"Yes; he was a delicate-looking man, and died young; you resemble him in a remarkable degree. Your father was a good man, Isabella, and was much attached to you, his only child.”

“I have often fancied he used to kiss me, sir: do men ever kiss their little girls?”

Isabella was looking into Father Martin’s eyes, now; asking him a seemingly absurd question, with the simplicity of a child of six. And she was fourteen years old. The kind-hearted priest turned away from her questioning glance for very pity, lest she should observe the effect her words had caused.

“Certainly, Isabella, they do. I have often seen your father kiss you. Why should he not have done so, as well as your mother?”

“My mother never kissed me in my life,” said Isabella, simply.

“Your mother was peculiar; that may have been the reason; but she was very good, — she meant well.”

“Was she, Father Martin? I don’t know; I am afraid I don’t understand things very well. I do not believe I am good. I think you are."

Pleased with her frankness, and touched by her painful simplicity and ignorance of all the sweet ministrations and joys of childhood, Father Martin saw, that to continue the subject, would be to set himself adrift upon an almost shoreless sea. In the home to which she was going she would learn the amenities of affection and kindness, and he smiled kindly as he answered, —

"I am far from being what I should be, my dear child; but I must inform you that your father's brother became a Catholic in the course of time, and in his turn saw the beauty of the true faith, and of its system of religious education. If your mother had lived, she would have placed you at a convent school next year; as it is, you will go immediately. My housekeeper, or better, perhaps, my sister, will see that you have everything you need, and I presume you can be ready in a week's time."

"Very well, father," said Isabella, without manifesting any sign of interest in the proposed change.

"For the present you will remain here with Mary. She has been a faithful servant, and your mother did not forget her. She has left her two hundred dollars in her will."

"She is very cross and stingy," said Isabella; "I do not like her."

Father Martin passed his hand across his lips.

"That is owing to her age and infirmities, no doubt," he answered.

"Was my mother rich, Father Martin; I thought none but rich people made their wills?"

"Any one who has something to leave behind her may make a will in her own right; but you will have considerable money. Your uncle's legacy amounts to about ten thousand dollars; this house is worth fifteen hundred, and the interest of some railroad stocks left to your mother by her first husband, Mr. Pettigrew, will amount to about five or six hundred dollars."

"That is a great deal of money. Will you take care of it for me?"

"Father Boyce, Mr. Arthur Hanlon and myself were appointed by your mother for that purpose, Isabella. We will see that you are properly clothed and educated; and that your money is safely and profitably invested until you are of age. After that you will be at liberty to do as you please with it."

"Thank you, sir, I would rather go to a school where I should not be obliged to talk to the other girls. Do you think you could find one for me?"

"Such a school should be and is the farthest from my desires, Isabella. You would grow selfish and morose, if left entirely to your own thoughts and tastes. You have hitherto lived apart from young people of your own age, but now you must endeavor to conquer your aversion to society."

"Well, father, you know best; but I feel strange and lonely in a crowd; girls never like me, and I do not like boys."

"That will all come right in time, Isabella. At the end of a year, I have no doubt you will think otherwise."

After a few incidental questions on the part of Father Martin, the interview ended, and that day week, after bidding farewell to old Mary, who, much to her surprise, shed tears at parting with her, Isabella found herself sitting opposite Father Martin and Mr. Hanlon, in the last-named gentleman's carriage, rolling over a smooth turnpike road, farther away from Baltimore than she had ever been in her short, uneventful life. At the expiration of a couple of hours, passed in almost complete silence by the young girl, Father Martin bade her look out of the window to catch the first glimpse of her home.

The house stood on a high hill, in the midst of a plantation of fine trees, and was accessible only by a steep and winding road. Just now, in the blaze of the setting sun, its many-paned and numerous windows looked like burnished gold, and the gilt spire that crowned the gothic chapel of grey stone in the background, sparkled as though touched with pencilled points of fire. They were still at the foot of the mountain, but through the thick growth of trees and shrubbery, Isabella caught the echo of the young voices and merry laughter, and as they drove slowly up the ascent, the flutters of blue dresses among the firs made a pretty contrast to their sombre green. About half way from the gate they passed a beautiful shrine, and the grounds in front of the house were tastefully laid out with flowers. A group of small children were seated on the steps that led to the main entrance; but at sight of the carriage they tripped slyly away. Something of pleasure, mingled with curiosity, spoke from Isabella's eyes as she met Father Martin's kindly glance.

"It is a recreation-day, Isabella," said Father Martin; "you will have a good opportunity to become acquainted with your companions on this account."

She returned his kindly glance with a pleasant smile, but did not reply.

"Here we are;" said Mr. Hanlon, as the carriage driver opened the door, and in a few moments more Isabella and the two gentlemen were seated in the parlor, awaiting the entrance of the Lady Superior.

.   .   .   .

"How do you like the new boarder, Sybilla?" asked the tallest of a group of several girls, turning to the one beside her.

"I haven't thought much about her," replied the other; "she is very quiet, don't you think so?"

"Quite glum, is what I should call her," said a third; "she never speaks to any of us, and looks as though she thought we wanted to bite her."

"She has just lost her mother, Annie," said the first speaker, "and it is natural for her to feel lonely."

"But she is such a cross-looking thing, Flora. One needn't be cross, even if one is in trouble; particularly when people try to be friendly."

"Have you been trying to be friendly, Annie?" said Flora, smiling.

"Yes, of course, I have. Sister told me to show the new scholar to-morrow's lesson, and I did. After that I thought I would be real nice, you know, for I felt sorry for her, she looked so blue. So I said, 'Won't you come out and walk in the avenue?' And what do you think she said?"

"I'm sure I can't tell," answered Flora; "what was it?"

"'No!' plain 'no' without even a smile."

"Poor thing," said Flora; "she is a little odd, I think, but she does not look cross to me. Perhaps she has never been with so many girls before, and may be very shy. I think she is. I know how lonely and out of place I felt for the first day or two. There she comes now, with Sister Anselm. Let us go to meet them."

The girls went forward and Sister Anselm said kindly, as she released Isabella's hand:

"Young ladies, Isabella has not seen the shrine. You will have time to show it to her before the bell rings. Flora, I commit her to your charge; you must try and make her feel at home."

Flora put her arm around Isabella, and the kindness of the action was not unnoticed by the lonely girl. She raised her eyes with a look that meant " thank you," and the girls turned towards the leafy glade, some walking leisurely, others skipping gaily down the path. Isabella and Flora fell behind the rest, and when some moments had been passed in silence, Flora said:

" You have been here a week to-day, I believe. Do you like the convent?"

" It is a very large house, and handsomely built," answered Isabella.

" I did not mean the building, but the Sisters and the girls, and the way the school is conducted."

" I don't think I know more than two or three of the Sisters; but I like them. You and two or three others are the only girls

that have spoken to me out of school
hours.”

“ They are. a little timid about making
advances. You don’t seem to want to make
friends; you are so quiet and ·reserved;”
said Flora, drawing her arm close around
the slender figure; “ no doubt you feel
lonely,” she continued, “ but if you once
make up your mind to be contented, I think
you will not find it hard. We are all very·
happy here.”

“ I do not feel lonely,” answered Isabella,
“ I feel strange. I have never been with
other girls much. My mother did not like
me to play with children; she thought they
were foolish. I am not used to playing
games like the girls play here.”

“ You will soon become accustomed to
our ways, Isabella,” said Flora; “ we are a
little noisy, but you will not mind that, in
time, either.”

“ Oh, I don’t mind it at all. But you are
not noisy. I like to see you walk across the
floor.”

Flora laughed. "I am more than sixteen, Isabella; too old to be noisy."

"I am fourteen, but I never was noisy, I think. Do you like to read poetry?"

"Yes, why do you ask?"

"That girl with the light curls told me you were the poetess of the school. She said you wrote acrostics. I know what they are, I have read about them in my Encyclopædia. Will you write one for me?"

Flora's face reddened, and she looked a little confused as she answered,—

"I do write verses sometimes, but it is generally when there is some entertainment on hand. But I wish the girls would not say it of me."

"I think I should like it, — I mean to be able to write poetry. Will you write some for me to-day, when I can see you? I have never seen any one writing poetry."

"Yes, if it pleases you; but I can't do much. Here we are at the shrine. Isn't it beautiful?"

Within a delicately carved trellis work,

canopied and shaded by a wreath of vines
and flowers, was a statue of the Madonna,
holding the Infant Jesus in her arms. The
attitude and expression were perfect, and a
gentle hush fell upon the lively group as
they knelt on the outer step for a moment
to offer up a fervent Hail Mary. Tears
were trembling in Isabella's eyes when she
arose.

"I think it is very easy to be good here,"
she said aloud. Then turning to Flora, she
continued : "You are the best girl in school ;
she told me," looking at Annie, who blushed
like fire.

A subdued titter ran through the group
of girls ; and Flora, forgetting her own
embarrassment, in the fear that Isabella
might feel hurt at the thoughtlessness of
the rest, drew her away from the steps, saying,—

"Annie talks at random sometimes. We
had better get back to the playground before
the bell rings."

But Isabella had noticed the laugh at her

expense, and not conscious of having given any cause for merriment, she said, in a choking, hurried voice,—

" Why do they laugh at me?   I said what was true.   She did tell me so, and I believe it ; you are the only one who did not laugh. I like you ; but I shall not talk to the others any more."

" Oh, Isabella, do not say that," answered Flora, leading her into a by-path ; " they did not intend to hurt your feelings, and they laughed to see Annie look confounded. They were a little surprised at your frankness, too."

" I will stay by myself after this," said Isabella ; " I am not used to girls like that. At the school where I went in Baltimore, I never played with the rest ; my mother would not let me, and I suppose I am different from other people."

" Oh, no, you are not, Isabella.   We are not allowed to go by ourselves, here, and it is a wise rule.   We don't have a chance to grow discontented or unhappy."

"I am not unhappy," said Isabella, fixing her eyes on the ground.

"But you are not very happy, are you? You do not feel like running and skipping; and you don't care to join the others at recreation, do you?"

"I am too tall and old to run and skip," answered Isabella, almost laughing, "but I never feel like it, either."

"I am taller and older than you, and I often take a run down the hill in the morning and evening," said Flora.

"My mother used to scold me when I screamed, or ran down stairs fast; she said it was like a tom-boy. Have you got a mother?"

Flora never forgot the tone in which Isabella uttered these words, and in them she read the sorrowful experience of a short lifetime. It was as though she had asked: "Have you a persecutor? Or, you seem so happy, you cannot have a mother."

Her heart warmed to the strange, friendless girl, as she answered,—

"Yes, indeed I have, and the best mother

any one ever had. I am sure you would love her if you knew her."

"Have you a father, too?" asked Isabella, in a soft tone.

"Yes, and two dear little sisters, and a great, tall brother."

"I think I should have loved my father," said Isabella earnestly, "I am sure you are happy."

The ringing of the bell brought the conversation to a sudden close, and the girls went to the different class rooms. At the evening recreation, many of them had remarks to make on the "odd behavior" of the new girl, to whom, however, they did not give equal credit for acute observation or sensitiveness.

But she saw that they considered her peculiar, and kept aloof from them as much as possible. After supper, Flora brought her out of the corner in which she had hidden herself, and they walked up and down the corridor together, until the bell rang for night prayers.

The next day, Flora contrived to make Isabella the centre of a group of the largest girls, who were just beginning Algebra. The previous evening, she had discovered Isabella's penchant for that study, and almost before she knew it, she found herself talking interestedly and without embarrassment. Sister Anselm joined them after a while, and Isabella felt quite contented when she was by, for the kind sister had attracted the child's heart at first sight.

For some time it was difficult to draw Isabella from the reserve which long habit and the forced repression of her feelings, had rendered almost natural. And the apathy and silence to which her former surroundings had accustomed her, were very often mistaken by her companions for indifference and coldness. But Flora, who had read the girl's heart on the day of the visit to the shrine, understood her better, and although young and inexperienced herself, her intuition told her of hidden springs of warmth beneath the surface.

Beloved by all her teachers and companions, the fact of her adoption, as it were, of the poor child, went far towards making Isabella more popular than her own best endeavors could have done. Little by little, her shyness wore off; she became accustomed to her new life, and grew to like it; the repressed tenderness of her nature found many an outlet in mutual acts of kindness, and she had not been a year at the convent before she was a general favorite.

She became deeply attached to Flora in particular, to whom much of the credit of the happy change was due. Father Martin expressed great pleasure at her satisfaction and improvement, and delighted her one morning by telling her she had grown wonderfully like her father.

The year drew to a close, Flora's last at school, and a few evenings before the Distribution day, she and Isabella were walking in the garden, near the shrine.

"Do you remember the first time we came here together, Flora," said Isabella, "and how the girls laughed when I spoke of your being better than the rest?"

"Yes, I have never forgotten it. I felt sorry for you that day you seemed so lonely."

"And I was lonely, although I did not know it myself. You opened my heart."

"Don't pay any compliments to-day, Isabella; you gave me enough then to last for two years."

"I do think you write pretty verses, Flora; I will keep that Acrostic as long as I live."

"In another year you will be one of the largest girls," said Flora, "and my verse writing will not do me much good in the world, I am afraid."

"Oh, yes, it may; you can write for the magazines and papers, and I'm sure they'll all be glad to have whatever you send them."

Flora laughed merrily. "You'll be getting romantic next, Isabella," she said.

By this time they had reached the shrine.

The setting sun was throwing its slanting rays athwart the thick nasturtium vines that shaded the enclosure, and the sweet breath of blossoming honeysuckles came floating through the evening air.

"The dear, old Convent," said Flora, "and this blessed shrine. How strange it seems, to think that I am going to leave them forever."

"Do you know, Flora, I shall never come here without thinking of you?"

"And then you will always pray for me."

"Yes; and I never do come here, as it is, without thinking that"—she hesitated, and Flora looked at her inquiringly. "Well, I can't exactly say what I mean, but it seems to me that I shall always feel sorry for new girls, and try to make them get over their home-sickness. I might have been an icicle yet, if you had not been kind to me."

"Sister Anselm would have thawed you out, long before this," said Flora.

"May be so, but I don't know; I love her a very great deal, though."

Flora parted the boughs that hung over the entrance to the shrine, and once more they knelt together at the feet of the Madonna.

The angelus bell sounded from the village church down in the valley, and Flora repeated the angelical salutation, whilst Isabella responded aloud.

"Modest little shrine amid the trees; how many hearts remember you, with joy forever."

Dear girls, I was once a girl like you; school life, my world; my companions, its inhabitants, embracing as many different traits of character as though it was measured by miles, instead of one little acre, or perhaps not more than half so much. If this simple story bears a moral, let it read — that in the school-room world, which, all things told, is not so small, all can find good work to do; and though in every school there may be found Isabellas, there would not be one-half so many lonely, hidden, friendless hearts if there were many Floras.

THE MAY QUEEN.

I T was May Eve. The inhabitants of a picturesque hamlet in one of the Alpine cantons of Switzerland had donned their holiday attire, and were gathered to celebrate, with dance and song, the recurrence of their favorite *fete*. The maire has invited them to his pretty chalet, and before the open windows, on the gentle ascent commanding a view of the snow-clad hills beyond the silvery lake, the musicians play the introductory music, and dancing is commenced.

"It is too soon, too soon yet," cried one of the assembly; "you should wait till our Queen is chosen."

The dissent caused the music to cease, and the dancers to stand idly for a moment, when, suddenly, all are startled by the thrilling sweetness of a voice, which, with a strange unearthly cadence in its depths, entoned the following words : —

"She who in weakness hath nursed Him,
Who with Him in exile hath been,
Who 'neath the cross did not falter,
Alone is our festive Queen."

A silence as of death fell on the merry-makers. The fervent solemnity of the unexpected utterance pierced their hearts. They all at once felt that a higher and nobler purpose than their own amusement must have drawn them together, and their souls were lifted up by the opportune reminder. The gaze of all was riveted on a figure in the open balcony, which filled them with a holy awe and reverence, such as might be inspired by a vision from heaven itself.   It was that of a young girl of fifteen, clad in a long, clinging robe of spotless white, with a bodice of pale blue, and a sash of the same tint, hanging down almost to her feet. Her head was uncovered, and her luxuriant hair floated over her shoulders.   Her short sleeves displayed arms pure and white as those of an infant; and her beautiful features, irradiated with the inspiration of her song, had a look in them of the celestial home to which she was evidently hastening. Her large eyes shone with a strange light, her red lips were apart, and the hectic flush on her cheeks deepened, as she gazed with encouraging love on the upturned faces of the villagers.   Some of the older wept, but the younger ones shouted aloud, "It is Marie, it is Marie, and she must be our Queen!"

"Yes, yes," was the general exclamation, "Marie shall be the Queen of the May!"

Marie, the only and beloved daughter of the village maire, was her father's pride, and the idol of all who knew her.   Consumption had laid its fatal hold upon her, and it was in compliance with her express desire that her companions has been bidden hither this evening, that she may witness the festival.

"Yes, yes," was the re-echoed cry; "Marie shall be our May Queen. Her crown, her crown!"

It was brought, a wreath of fair, white lilies displayed on a blue cushion. Two young girls were chosen to ascend the outer stairs and place it on her young head. This done, they knelt before her, according to the festive wont, to offer the regal salutation; but they could only clasp her hands in theirs and burst into tears. She smiled brightly, and stooping forward, kissed their foreheads, and sent, as their queen, a command to those below to resume their merry-making.

Scarcely had they regained their companions when again the voice of Marie sang out in unearthly sweetness the conclusion of her hymn:—

"Fain would I remind you of Mary,
Her, only who spotless hath been;
At her feet I'll lay all your homage,
She alone is our May-day Queen."

In obedience to Marie's behest, the amusement went on more heartily than ever; but they celebrated the May-eve no longer as a mere custom, but in honor of her who is the Queen of Heaven and of the sweet May month.

The festivities had come to a close. The night-stars glimmered in the moonless sky, when a sudden brilliancy illuminated the balcony, from which their May Queen had been smiling down upon her dutiful subjects. They looked up, and beheld Marie reclining in an attitude of calm repose. A crucifix was clasped to her heart, and on her head the crown of lilies glistened in their whiteness. The smile of love still peacefully lingered on her lips, but her pure spirit had soared to heaven. Their May Queen was dead.

FATHER IS COMING.

"HUSH, Nellie; father is coming."

There was an instant hush in the merry laugh of the golden-haired Nellie; the sweet smile died away from her lips, and a chill, as of ice, passed over her heart.

And all because "Father is coming." Mr. Parker kept the sunshine to garnish his office, and brought home the clouds to darken his home.

The art of making home happy, is greater than the art of gaining wealth or honor or position. It is one seldom learned or appreciated. It had not been learned by Mr.

Parker. No; he had been too much engrossed in gathering up riches to heed the
pleadings of the hearts of those who, gathered about the home circle, watched and
waited his coming, as the inhabitants of the
Arctic zone watch the coming of the sun.
And when, instead of bright eyes and sunny
beams, there fell upon the hearth-stone
harsh looks and cold responses, do you
wonder that the dreariness of home was
made still more drear, and the bounding
heart became chilled by their influence?

"Father is coming."

"Is he?"

"Yes! Shut the picture book and lay
aside the playthings. No more laughter or
innocent mirth now."

Mr. Parker had not always been so. In
fact he still was, as of old, the kind provider,
and even most attentive to the wants of his
family. He surrounded his wife with all the
luxuriance that wealth and taste could obtain, and even prided himself on the comforts he was daily showering on her.

But there was a painful comparison in the mind of that wife as she watched the fluttering of a golden-winged canary in its gilded cage. The sense of imprisonment was keenly felt. The bird was fed and kept in royal slavery. And how much better was she than the bird before her? How the change came would be difficult to narrate. Doubtless it was not intentional, but was no less effective. All this while no cross words were spoken except by the eyes and conduct of the husband. And Agnes, as she saw how indifference was gradually taking the place of love; as she watched the complete engrossment of her husband's mind in his business, grieved in her heart at the bleak prospect before her. So grew up a partial estrangement of heart. Their sympathies were not in common, their feelings were not the same. Not they were wanting in husbandly duty and wifely faith. But there was a link, once possessed, but now lost.

But the lost link? Where was it? Under

what rubbish of years did it lay hid? "Father is coming."

As he entered, the mother whispered to Nellie, and the child leaves the room. She returns in a moment and makes some reply. Mr. Parker looks on but says nothing.

"Dinner will soon be served," said his wife in answer to the thought that evidently engrossed his attention at that moment.

He seated himself by the window, picked up a paper and commenced reading.

A few minutes passed in silence, each busy with their own thoughts.

He was vexed at the delays; she, conscious of giving no offence, was irritated at his morose manner, gave up all ideas of conciliatory measures, and so widened the breach, At last the dinner bell sounded.

The meal was soon over, Mr. Parker arose from the table, took his hat, and was about leaving when his wife asked,—

" What time will you be home this evening? "

" I cannot tell," was the response. " My

business may detain me longer than usual. Why do you ask the question?"

"I thought of taking Nellie out to see Aunt Eunice."

"Well, you can be home when I return."

"If I knew what hour you would come up, yes."

Mr. Parker paused. Then remarking "Well, be home early, at any rate," left the room.

The uncertainty of the reply almost tempted Mrs. Parker to adhere to her intention, and pay the visit contemplated. For a moment she pondered over it, and then her good angel triumphed. She would remain at home even at the sacrifice of the pleasure of Nellie. The child heard the decision; if it brought a tear to her eye we need not wonder, and in the heartache of one the other joined,—

"Never mind, mother, I can wait."

"Thanks, darling," was all the mother could reply.

Early evening came, but no Mr. Parker. His wife patiently waited.

The hour went on. Still he came not. On the sofa Nellie lay, her golden hair falling over her face — asleep. She had grown weary watching. The mother, too, sat in an easy chair by the side of the centre table, endeavoring to read. But the words ran into one another, and she was forced to close the book, and as her head dropped upon her hand, and there came the vision of the years when every cloud had a rainbow, she contrasted the happy " then " to the unhappy " now," and sighed over her condition. She learned the lesson that wealth does not confer peace ; that gold cannot purchase happiness.

Her eyelids softly closed, and sleep — " best boon to mortals given " — came to her in her grief and waved her soothing wings over her perturbed heart. And as she slept she must have dreamed sweet dreams ; for a smile played over lips and she murmured : " Love me, love," as though of old a sweet confession was being made.

The door opened and Mr. Parker entered. He paused just as the threshold was crossed, and gazed for a few moments on the picture before him. It was one worthy the pencil of a master-painter.

And, as he paused, Nellie speaks. But she does not move. Mr. Parker listens.

"Mother, mother, why don't papa love us? Why don't he smile as he used to do? Mother — mother, why don't — he — love —"

The low voice of Nellie died away, and the heart of the father is smitten as with a rod. Truly conscience asks why? Nellie still sleeps. So does her mother. And as husband and father draws nearer to them again a smile played about the lips of his wife, and again she murmurs, "Love me, love."

Mr. Parker is on his knees. He takes the hand of Agnes in his own. She awakes with a loud cry of surprise, but as she hears the words, "Forgive, my long suffering, yet patient Agnes," she buries her face in his bosom. Nellie, too, awakes, and is added to the group. And as she wonders, and looks with smiling eyes from the face of one to the other, she feels that something must have happened while she slept.

Truly, something had happened. The link had been found, and to it a little child had led them.